INFESTATION

A HAUNTED SPACE NOVEL

Ryan M. Williams

GLITTERING THRONG PRESS | RAINIER WA

Glittering Throng Press
PO BOX 179 RAINIER WA 98576-0179
glitteringthrongpress.com

eBook ISBN-13 978-1-946440-65-5
Paperback ISBN-13 978-1-946440-64-8

GTP NO. 18

Contents

Chapter 1

L IFE IN THE UNCANNY valley was hard. And if anyone knew that, it was Jules, because of his prosthetic face. The looks he got–like he had something on his face–were bad enough until he remembered that it *was* his face. Not something on it.

Like the woman across the corner of the bar from him. Jules had noticed her the instant she came in. Curvy, not too short, skin showing a faint genuine bronze from someone that spent time under actual sunlight. Darker freckles in a constellation across her nose. Red hair going to blond at the tips, long so it flowed down past her shoulders in straight lines. And a fringe above shapely eyebrows. He loved a good fringe. When she'd leaned on the bar to order a drink from Dixon, Jules had seen that she had killer green eyes. She wore black pants, a matching tank that showed off the muscles in her arms. Only visible tech was a discreet node behind her right ear, matte black that could have been a shadow beneath her hair if he hadn't seen the power signature overlaid on his heads-up display.

She ordered an orange juice, took the stool as she scanned those present. He felt the intensity of her gaze on him and looked up to make eye contact. He offered a friendly tilt of his head.

She visibly recoiled, then squinted at him. It was life in the uncanny valley. His prosthetic face looked human enough, good-looking even, but then there was something about it that didn't look *quite right.* It made people uneasy. Human or alien, made no difference. Everyone was uncomfortable with it. He'd be uncomfortable with it too if he had to look in a mirror, so he didn't. And then forgot until he got that look again.

He broke eye contact with the woman and focused on his drink instead. Nonalcoholic fruit juice with ice, sugar, and *bounce.* He'd heard someone describe *bounce* as chocolate with kick once. He hadn't ever tasted chocolate, so he didn't know if it was a good comparison or not. He knew the important thing–*bounce* helped keep him sane. It kept the pain in his face to a level he could handle.

Dixon's place had a relaxed vibe to it. The light panels on the walls and ceiling kept the place in a soft glow with a hint of pink to it. Dixon said it helped keep people calm. Jules didn't know if that was the case or not, but fights rarely happened. The patrons appreciated the quiet atmosphere and helped keep it that way. Sometimes that meant an asshole would be offered one last drink before they went on their way. Usually that worked, with a few slurred curses on the way out.

Patrons at Dixon's were a mix of humans and other species. It didn't matter to anyone unless you sat on a chair recently occupied by either a retelorous (because of the spines) or a gierian (because of the slime). Dixon had a good bot crew, though that stayed busy bussing tables and cleaning up any messes whether they were biological or not.

It also wasn't a spacer's bar, those being located in the outer top or bottom ring. Central ring catered more to permanent residents on the station. Or those here on an extended stay like Jules.

Either way, people of any species came to Dixon's to relax, have a bite to eat, and be able to talk to their companions without shouting. It wasn't, though it happened from time to time, a place to go to hook up with someone. There were easier places to find companionship, a fact that suited Jules just fine. The looks aside, he could drink in peace at Dixon's without someone asking him about his face. Or the bone spirit beads braided in his hair, marking him as a medium.

He lifted his glass and studied the sparkling blue liquid coating the ice. The blue came from the fruit. Something from a binary planet, if he remembered right. Distilled down to an extract into a mild stimulant and flavor enhancer. The bright sparks that swirled in the drink? That was the *bounce*, from another plant that grew in the twilight regions of a tidally locked planet around an F-type star. The two were brought together with comet ice and water, sugar extracted from an Earth plant, and all of it blended to create his drink. Something that could never have existed without the technology to travel between different stars.

Jules took a drink and held it in his mouth. The flavors crawled like electricity over his tongue. *That* was original equipment, unlike his face, eyes, and ears. It was one sense that he could count on matching his expectations. The fruit gave the drink a bit of tartness balanced against the sugar and the kick of the *bounce*. His nerves practically sang with the pleasure of it as he savored the taste. The *bounce* was absorbed directly into his bloodstream through his tissues and made its way to his brain by the shortest paths available. As his mind woke to the *bounce*, he swallowed.

It helped. His mind expanded and the pain receded in proportion. It was the one thing that worked. Nothing else the neurologists had suggested worked as well.

Dixon stopped in front of Jules, another glass in his hand. Jules looked at it, his enhanced vision identifying the contents of the glass as the same beverage he was nursing.

He looked up at Dixon. The owner and bartender of the establishment was old, human, and bald with a pronounced hook at the end of his nose. He wore his usual red shirt with black apron and pants. The lines around his pale blue eyes deepened as he put the drink down.

"From the red-haired lady across the way, as an apology for her slight, I believe," Dixon said, his voice a quiet rasp from scarred lungs.

Dixon understood pain. It helped in his profession.

It took Jules a second to realize who Dixon meant. The woman was too attractive, her response too common, for Jules to think that much of it. He'd already dismissed it from his thoughts.

The drink forced him to look up again across the bar. She made eye contact again and this time smiled with what looked like real warmth. Her lips quirked a bit in what might signify embarrassment and apology.

Fine. Jules could take it. He touched the glass and gave her a nod to indicate his thanks.

Then he turned his attention back to his first drink. He took a bigger mouthful this time, now that he had a second drink waiting. He watched his drinking and his budget. It wouldn't do to let either get out of hand given the irregular nature of his income.

The extra surge of *bounce* in his system made him feel awake and aware of everything around him. The pain faded into the background like the sound of a noisy duct. There, but you got used to it.

With the next drink, he sucked in an ice cube and let it sit icily cold against his tongue as it melted. Water billions of years old, mined from comets in the system, and then recycled through the systems and people of the station over and over again. From water back to ice and now back to water.

"I wanted to apologize for any offense," a richly textured voice said in an accent that wasn't a station dialect.

Jules looked up from his drink to his right. The red-haired woman perched on the stool beside him, leaning closer on the bar. There was a sort of herbal scent about her he couldn't identify. Her intensely green eyes moved, studying his face up close.

Jules sighed. She was going to ask him about it. He shouldn't have accepted the drink. It'd encouraged her. Made her curious.

He turned his focus back to his drink and tipped it back, swallowing instead of savoring it. He put the glass with the ice down on the bar and slid back off his stool. He caught Dixon's eye and lifted a hand in a farewell gesture.

It was a shame to leave the other drink, but there it was.

Jules started out of the bar. His brain was already processing everyone around him, assessing them in case anyone was with the woman. It wouldn't be the first time that someone had tried to grab him, though it was rare. Mediums were always in demand, but few people resorted to abduction.

None looked like a threat. He nodded to a couple regulars on his way out. The woman had also left the bar.

His ears told him that much, and his sense of smell. She was following him out, hurrying to catch up.

He hadn't expected that. Most people would have been offended and let him go without trouble.

If she followed him out of the bar he might have to call station police. He didn't want to, but he wasn't going to let her follow him home.

Chapter 2

J ULES HEARD A CHAIR scuff behind him and voices. Then her voice, the red-haired woman, carried clearly to his ears.

"Mr. Moon, please. I only want a few words."

He stopped at the threshold. *She knew who he was.* Not that there were likely to be that many people with a prosthetic face and bone spirit beads in their hair. Outside the bar, people of many species and droids moved along the central ring. Some at work, others shopping, enjoying the company of friends, or hurrying off home after work. Lines of people formed outside the transfer pod station a short distance downspin. He'd have to wait in that line to catch a car that would take him out to the council housing. If he didn't talk to her now, she'd be able to catch up to him while he waited for the car.

Jules turned around. A small group of regulars were blocking the woman's path, gestures suggesting that she return to the bar for a drink. They were doing their best to intercede without being directly confrontational. Seeing that he had stopped and turned, the solicitations died away. A couple of the human patrons looked a bit disappointed.

Jules walked back a couple steps and people started drifting away, back to their tables. Still out of arm's reach, he said, "Bar."

He walked past her, keeping a courteous distance.

"Maybe we should talk somewhere more private?" she said, in that accent he didn't recognize.

"Bar," he said, and continued back to his seat.

Dixon was already there, Jules's second drink still in the same spot where he'd left it. Jules slid into his seat, meeting Dixon's eyes.

The older man grinned. His eyes flicked past Jules's shoulder. "Need anything else?"

Jules shook his head.

He caught her faint herbal scent, a lotion, perhaps, as she slid onto the stool next to him.

He picked up the glass. "You've got until I finish my drink. Then I'm gone."

"I apologize for my reaction when I saw you," she said. "I knew, but–"

"You knew?" He looked over the glass at her, deliberately making eye contact. Readouts overlaid themselves onto what he was seeing, showing details about her respiration, heart rate, temperature, and pupil dilation. With a thought, he dismissed the readouts. It was distracting and he'd seen enough. She was anxious, but not overly so. Embarrassed. Maybe afraid her mistake would be a problem.

"I knew," she said. "I came here looking for you."

He took a drink, barely savoring the flavor, and emptied nearly a third of the glass. Ice clinked when he set it down.

"Why?"

"Something is happening to my family. Something we can't explain. I think we're being haunted. I read that you help people with that sort of thing?"

It was worse than he'd thought. *She came to him about a haunting?* He took another long drink. When he put the glass down, less than a third remained. It was mostly ice.

"Usually there's a rational explanation," he said. "Old ventilation systems. Faulty or degraded circuits. Buggy or hacked software. You need experts to look at whatever is happening."

"That's why I came to you," she said. She kept her voice low. "Please. I have two daughters and they're terrified. We all are. Won't you take a look?"

Jules tipped the glass, rotating it between his fingers. She sounded sincere. He didn't bother opening his readouts. There wasn't much point.

He sighed, picked up the drink, and drained the glass. *Bounce* ignited his nerves as it coated his tongue and throat.

Her face fell when he put the glass down. Then she looked up and met his gaze. He smiled, knowing that his too-perfect smile rarely comforted anyone. She didn't recoil this time.

"What's your name?" he said.

"Briana Makkar." Her eyes began to water. "You'll help us?"

Jules interlaced his fingers, his elbow leaning on the bar. "I can't say that yet. Not until I know more about what's going on. But I'll listen and take a look."

"Oh, thank you. That's wonderful. We've been so scared. Teegan, my wife, is with the girls."

"Where are you docked?"

She shook her head. "We're not. We don't have a berth here. I hired a transport ship to bring me to the station."

Jules nodded. That wasn't a surprise, given what he'd heard. The system was littered with vessels scraping by one way or another. Berth fees being what they were, many ships wouldn't dock with the station if they could do anything to avoid it. Too expensive and if you fell behind on your dock fees, your whole ship could end up impounded until you could pay your debt. If you couldn't, you might end up with your ship sold right out from under you.

He'd already seen her tech. He sent a connection ping to her system feed. Her mouth parted as she looked at, then accepted the invite. He saw the acknowledgment when he was added to her contacts.

"Arrange transport for tomorrow," he said. "I have some things I need to put together before then. Send me the transport details when you have them. I'll meet you there."

"Thank you so much, Mr. Moon."

"Jules," he said. "Just Jules."

She nodded. "Okay. Call me Bri, everyone does."

"Bri. I'll see you tomorrow."

He slid of the stool and walked away. She watched him go, he felt her gaze on him, but didn't make any move to follow.

Usually these sorts of reports meant nothing at all. Like he'd told Bri, wiring or ventilation problems accounted for most disturbances.

As he passed the regulars that had helped stop her he said, with a ping to Dixon, "Next round is on me."

That earned him appreciative smiles and a few soft words of thanks. He raised a hand and walked out of the bar.

Church first, he decided.

Chapter 3

T HE TRIP TO CHURCH passed uneventfully. Jules pulled up his hood as he merged with the crowd outside of Dixon's and made his way to the station. He purchased a shared ticket to the nearest station and boarded with three other passengers in the car. Two other humans, an older male-female couple, holding hands and moving with care as they took the forward-facing seats on one side of the car. Retirees, he thought, from their casual dress and relaxed postures. Probably out to get something to eat.

The third person on the pod was a short droid, dome top, cylindrical body supported magnetically above the deck. It kept its multiple arms neatly folded up against its body out of the way as it floated after the couple into the pod. It took up a position at the back, to the other side. No telling what the droid did. It might work for the station or some other business. Could even be from a spacer ship. The blue and orange markings didn't give away anything to Jules.

He stepped into the pod and reached up to grab the rail above the door, turning to face the door as it closed. He turned his head slightly away from the couple.

The pod moved smoothly off through the transfer station, merging into the line and accelerating smoothly. It wasn't far to the next station, two minutes later the pod reached the station and stopped. Jules stepped out the instant the doors opened.

Clayton was one of the older neighborhoods on the station. It was an agricultural and residential segment. Buildings rose up around Central street, the tallest nearly reaching the top of the segment. Four blocks over to 1st Street, or four blocks south to 8th Street, and the buildings gave way to the vertical farms that produced fresh food for the station and trade with spacers.

Jules didn't go that way. Instead, he headed downspin along Central eight blocks until he came to Central Park. Then over two blocks to 6th Street and Park Avenue where the church steeples rose up toward the segment ceiling above.

Unlike the glass and steel of the buildings surrounding it, the St. Butler Cathedral was built of blocks of dark asteroid rock. Two steeples rose into sharp points on each side of the entrance. The grand doors were of pale wood grown right here on the station, bound with dark iron from asteroids. The massive stained-glass window above the entrance showed St. Butler's broad face looking down, her expression warm and welcoming. The patron saint of space, spacers, and stationers alike held out her hand, a bright green sapling coiling up into the sunlight that radiated around her head.

He had paused, looking at the stained-glass image as he always did, drawing strength from the wisdom in her gaze. He bowed his head, looked up and climbed the slight ramp to the doors.

The air inside was cooler and tinged with incense and candle smoke. A droid attendant stood inside the narthex, robbed in a silky black fabric, cowl up over its elongated head. Blue lights gleamed from its animated features.

"St. Butler's blessings upon you," the droid said in a deep, somewhat raspy voice. "Be at peace."

It wasn't always easy to tell the attendants apart, but Jules's eyes picked up the faint pattern of scratches and wear on droid's head. His systems identified it for him.

"Nelson. How have you been?"

Nelson's animated face took on a smiling expression. "Well, Mr. Moon. We haven't seen you here for service lately. Are you well?"

"That's a complicated question," Jules said. "Is she available?"

"For confessions, yes," Nelson said. "I believe you know the way?"

Confessions. Jules nodded. "I do, thank you."

"You're very welcome."

Jules turned and left Nelson to their duties. Many droids like Nelson grappled with their beliefs and origins and found themselves drawn to the Butlerian Church of Universal Peace. The cathedral's high ceiling arched above, painted in a stunning mural of the known space-faring species against the backdrop of the galaxy. Each of the systems of origin depicted out of scale to show the details of those thirty-three worlds. The section occupied by the known species was only a small part of the galactic mural–showing how much more of the galaxy remained unknown. The Church anticipated growth and communication, envisioning an entire galaxy at peace.

Jules appreciated the vision, but found his focus remained more on the immediate future.

He crossed to the aisles along the nave and walked past the pews where some worshippers sat and contemplated St. Butler's teachings. It was mostly empty. There wasn't anyone waiting at the confessional.

Jules opened the panel door and stepped inside, pulling it closed behind himself. Through the mesh, he could just make out the outline of Mother Anna's shape.

"St. Butler's blessings on you," she said, her voice deep and resonant. "What brings you to confession today?"

"I am afraid, Mother. I find myself less at peace than I wish."

"What is the nature of your conflict?"

"I've been approached by a woman who says that her family is haunted. If it is true, I am afraid of what might happen."

Mother Anna shifted on her seat. She sighed. "Do you believe this intrusion is real?"

"Maybe," he said. "She went to considerable trouble to come here and find me."

"Where you given any indication of the source of this disturbance?"

"No, Mother. It may yet prove to have a more tangible explanation."

She made a sound that might have been a laugh. "Jules, if she convinced you, your instincts are rarely wrong in these cases. You came here today looking for inner peace before this trial."

It wasn't a question. And she was right. If he was going to face some sort of spiritual disturbance, he needed to be at peace with himself as much as was humanly possible.

"I have had uncharitable thoughts about others," he said. "I have lacked generosity. I have been selfish with my time and my self."

"I see," she said. "Then your penance is the task before you, to bring peace to those that sought your help. And if there is a spiritual disturbance, to bring peace to those on the other side."

"I will," he said.

"Then go with St. Butler's blessings on you, Jules. Nelson will supply you with blessed water, may it aid you in your task."

"Thank you, Mother. Blessings of St. Butler to you as well."

"Go in peace," Mother Anna said.

"Go in peace," Jules repeated.

He rose to his feet.

As he reached for the door, Mother Anna said, "Be careful Jules."

"I will," he said. He let himself out and found Nelson waiting outside with a black case.

"These are for you," Nelson said. "With St. Butler's blessings upon them."

"Thank you, Nelson," Jules said, taking the case. He touched the releases on the side and the lid lifted. Inside were a couple dozen small vials of virgin cometary water. Unprocessed water blessed by the Church and used in cleansing rituals. He closed the lid.

"You are most welcome," Nelson said. The droid bowed slightly and then walked away.

Jules tucked the case beneath his arm, glanced at the confessional, then started back down the aisle.

The Church's blessing helped if this turned out to be what Bri claimed. And if not? Hopefully the blessings would still help. He wasn't sure which outcome he dreaded more.

His steps slowed. *Why would he think that?* Obviously he didn't want Bri's family to be in danger. If he could identify a mundane explanation for what was happening–even if it was also dangerous–that should be the best outcome.

Except he knew that part of him that wanted to make the connection again to the other realm, beyond life. Places could become like reefs in the spiritual plane, infused with energy and an active spiritual ecosystem. Spaceships interacted with the very fabric of existence with the zero-point generators and dark matter collectors that made it possible to cross the expanding fabric of the universe. That sort of activity was known to fuel the spiritual ecosystem in some cases. It was like a bolt of electricity shooting across the universe. It ripped through spiritual ecosystems, but could also reinvigorate them. Especially at nexus points like a planet or station. Or even a spaceship. Most of the time the consequences were slight, unnoticeable. A healthy spiritual ecosystem helped support life, according to the Church.

Jules believed it could. He also knew what happened when things went badly wrong.

Chapter 4

AFTER LEAVING THE CHURCH, Jules took another car further downspin to the council housing district. He left the pod at the station and entered the crowds of people coming and going through the station's wide corridors.

He went with the flow and left the transit station for the streets. The main streets were wide, designed to handle many people of all sorts of species. Frequent roundabouts offered places to rest or gather. The first floor of the buildings rising on each side of the street were shops, various dining options, service businesses, and entertainment companies. The next six floors up were housing units which finally ended some distance above with the glowing panels of the sky.

It did resemble a city on a planet–if one ignored the inverted curve of the of street. Look far enough ahead and you could see the street curving up, plants, people, and buildings rising higher until the upward curve met the sky panels in the distance. The architecture of the buildings varied by the designer–not all human–except for the general height being the same. Some places had balconies, others didn't. The Pledian-designed buildings were covered with hexagonal landing portals from which they came and went a bit like puffy insects, each individual radiating their own unique bioluminescent patterns along their bodies and trailing tentacles. An inoffensive species that improved the décor with their colorful displays.

It was *home*. Not only for him, but for tens of thousands of other people of all species. The council housing was a public utility, like the air, water, power, and data connections. Residents were supplied with a basic income, medical care, and education. Those employed received a supplemental income from their employer. Or were self-employed. Jules had seen worlds where that basic shared care of individuals wasn't practiced and had seen the suffering it caused.

Not that they didn't have problems here, but there was a safety net for all beings. In an environment like the station, and even more so on a spaceship, that was important.

If Bri and her family had docked, and couldn't pay the docking fees, they could have lost their ship and would have ended up here, in council housing.

Wealthier individuals could afford housing in other districts where the station charged a housing tax. Or even, in the wealthiest districts, individuals could purchase station shares and become part of the council.

Spacers like Bri, though, valued their independence and their ability to go anywhere they wanted. Who wouldn't? Jules had lived that life for a long time, but that was in the past.

He brought his attention back to where he was and away from thoughts that remained painful. He was thinking about it, he knew, because he had said he would go with Bri. Leave the station. He hadn't done that in a long time either. There was plenty here for him to focus on.

But he needed to get some things from his place. And he needed to find MAR-A. He didn't work alone. He hadn't brought it up with Bri, but he needed to have MAR-A with him. It'd be easier to show up ready to leave with MAR-A then take time to explain.

He sent a quick text to MAR-A. "What're you doing? Can you meet me at my place? I've been offered a job."

MAR-A replied instantly. "On my way. You accepted without asking me. Again. Did you tell them you had a partner?"

"No," he said.

"Didn't want to scare them off with the combat droid?"

Yes. But Jules didn't send that. MAR-A already knew the answer. And knew that many people weren't that comfortable around the tall combat droid. Too much history in that reaperish silhouette. People who knew MAR-A had accepted the droid. Even cared about them.

Those who didn't know MAR-A sometimes ran screaming in the opposite direction.

"I'm almost home," he sent instead.

"Already there. I let myself in."

"Make yourself at home," Jules sent.

Which MAR-A would do, in their own way.

Jules reached his building a couple of minutes later. The resident entrance recognized him and let him in. He crossed the lobby and took the elevator up to the top floor. He exited and went down the bright corridor to his door. MAR-A hadn't broken it to get in. Not that they wouldn't if they thought it was necessary. Knowing MAR-A, it had been able to access the residence's systems and convinced it to let MAR-A enter. The building was, in its own way, as much of an artificial intelligence as MAR-A. He suspected that all of the AIs worked together when it suited them. He'd considered adding a primitive mechanical lock—but it wouldn't stop anyone determined about getting in. Especially not someone like MAR-A. And for the most part, break-ins were rare in council housing. Aside from the building security systems, no one really had anything that someone else would want. Basic levels of support helped more than policing at reducing crime. He knew that first hand, having seen places that didn't have that foundational safety net for residents. It didn't make sense, but that didn't seem to always matter.

The door opened for Jules, and he walked into a dim apartment. A tall shape loomed out of the shadows as the door closed. Dim metal reflections gleamed beneath the deep black cowl like coins placed over the eyes of the dead. A dark sleeve raised, metallic bony fingers clicked as they uncurled, pointing at him.

"Hey MAR-A," Jules said, looking up. "It doesn't work as well when I already knew you were here."

The apartment's light panels glowed to life and dispelled the shadows. MAR-A reached up with two long-fingered hands, and pulled back the cowl. The metal skull gleamed beneath the lights, complex etchings in the dark material created a pattern across their head. MAR-A's eyes pulsed with a faint blue light around the rim. From within the nightmarish figure came the dry, rattling sound of MAR-A's laughter. It was like fingers scratching in the grave of someone buried alive.

Terrifying, if you didn't know what it was.

"I scared you," MAR-A said in a raspy voice tinged with humor and a hint of hysteria.

Jules continued on into the room. "You didn't."

"Most beings would expel liquid waste if they saw me like that," MAR-A said.

"Some," Jules said, "are easily frightened."

MAR-A followed him. "What is this job you accepted without asking me?"

He sat the case with the blessed water down on the worktop, then went around to the refrigerator. He opened it and took out a juice.

When he turned around, MAR-A stood right behind him in his space. The big droid could move soundlessly when they wanted. Jules cocked his head to the side, looking up as he opened the juice.

MAR-A stepped back. "Scared you again."

"Keep telling yourself that." Jules tipped the bottle in their direction, then walked past to perch on one of the stools by the worktop.

He took a sip. It didn't have *bounce*, but it tasted sweet and quenched his thirst.

He said, "It's a family. Briana–goes by Bri– and Teegan Makkar. They have daughters, I don't have their names. According to Bri they are terrified by something haunting their ship."

"There's no docking registration with those names," MAR-A said, obviously having just searched, "but there is an entrance record for Briana Makkar. She has a ticket on an in-system transport leaving tomorrow."

Jules nodded. "They didn't bring their ship in. We have to meet it."

"I've secured passage for us on the same transport," MAR-A said.

"Forward–"

"I already shared the information with Briana Makkar using your codes."

"Thank you," Jules said. "It's nice that we work so well together."

"My modeling allows an 85% accuracy in predicting your general behavior. Anticipation of your decisions rises to over 90% in many circumstances."

"That's great for your modeling. Why do you keep trying to scare me if you can model that accurately?"

MAR-A's head lowered as it studied him. "It is an anomaly in the model."

Good. Jules sipped his juice and fought back a yawn. It was late, he was tired. He wanted to get some sleep before they ended up leaving tomorrow, but there was more work to be done. He took another sip and regretted that it lacked *bounce.*

Even caffeine would have been an acceptable substitute at this point.

MAR-A made a sound like claws in a boiling pot of water and straightened. "It should have worked."

"Keep telling yourself that," Jules said. "What do you have on the Makkar's ship?"

"Do I look like a library terminal?"

Jules raised an eyebrow and didn't answer.

MAR-A made a sound like metal being sharpened before saying, "Minimal details in the station's registry.

Only what is required for ships within the station's space. They stay out in the periphery, comet harvesters according to the registration. They aren't the original crew of the *Olympia*. They purchased it recently on a Station Association contract. Standard spacer records, for all the good that does."

"Spotty, huh?"

"Like blood splatters," MAR-A said. "Likely from out of the system, likely sank everything into the deal to buy the *Olympia*."

"How did the Station Association end up with the papers on the ship?"

"Bought from a salvage crew that reported the ship adrift and unoccupied. The Station Association made the usual attempts to track any relatives without results." MAR-A flexed their hands, making cracking noises. "It's likely that they didn't try too hard. The *Olympia* is a comet harvester ship. Could have drifted from the nearest system."

"Which is uninhabited."

MAR-A's dry, rattling laugh made it clear what the droid thought of that statement.

Jules shrugged. "Okay. So an independent comet harvester ship runs into trouble. Accidents happen. If it was bad enough that the crew died or evacuated, that could explain the haunting. Ship drifts and is caught in this system where a salvage crew finds it. Failing to find anyone to inherit, the Station Association sells it to the Makkar's, who probably think that this is their chance to live independnt of other spacers or the stations."

"Delusion humans," MAR-A said. "Inevitably, they must seek others with some pretext or another."

"Maybe," Jules said. He drained the juice and stood up. "I've got to get sleep before we ship out tomorrow. See you in the morning."

MAR-A stomped, making noise to show their displeasure, away from the worktop. They stood beside the couch for a moment, then folded down sitting back in the cushions. MAR-A's knees jutted up like two bony stakes. They crossed their arms and leaned back, eyes dimming to faint circles.

It was normal enough for MAR-A to behave that way. Jules put the juice bottle in the recycler and went to bed.

He woke suddenly in the dark. He still wore his prosthetic face. He hadn't heard anything, but he knew he was being watched. He didn't move, didn't need to move, as he looked at the time on his dim wall clock. Only two hours had passed. He looked into the dark shadows in the corner of his bedroom. Deep within the shadows was something darker, a shadow within a shadow. He was just able to make out the gleam of the eyes beneath the cowl.

"Are you going to watch me sleep?" Jules said.

"I scared you," gasped MAR-A's deathly voice from the shadows. "Scared you awake."

"Absolutely," Jules said. "And if you keep it up, I won't get any sleep tonight."

He rolled over, punching the pillow into shape. His ears detected the faintest rustle of robes as MAR-A stalked out of the room.

The droid mumbled in displeasure. "Anomalous human. Should be scared."

He couldn't be safer than with the big combat droid watching over him. Far from being scary, it was reassuring. Jules permitted himself a small smile and then let himself drift back off to sleep.

The Makkars might not find MAR-A as reassuring, at least at first.

Chapter 5

THE NEXT MORNING, JULES arrived at the transport dock early. His baggage bot squatted beside him with the few things he was bringing, clothes, packets of *bounce*, his exorcism kit, and the blessed water from the Church. He wore his usual outfit, hood pulled up to avoid the startled looks and stares from people seeing his face or the spirit beads in his hair. The baggage bot was programmed with a cheerful personality. It was a white oval shape, two sensor bands around its body, with a domed top that rotated out of the way for packing large items. Other panels opened to compartments for smaller items. It had retractable arms, at least four, that it used when packing belongings. Though he didn't have anything especially valuable, it would also keep his belongings secure.

He wasn't alone in the waiting area at the transport docks. The vessel had two passenger ports and a commercial cargo port further up spin from the passenger area. All of them were closed at the moment and fifty or or passengers waited in the area for boarding to begin. Humans accounted for about a third of the people gathered. The others were droids and a number of other species. He saw a fael, legs folded beneath it on the waiting area bench. A couple gierian pooled in a depression in the floor in apparent boredom. No one was paying any attention to him where he sat, hands clasped in front of him.

MAR-A lurked in a corner past the passenger dock. Anyone seeing the tall shape shrouded in hood and robe there made a hasty retreat. So all of the seats nearby remained empty.

Typical behavior from the combat droid. Find a place where it could put its back against a wall, and then scan the area for any potential signs of trouble.

Many of the passengers would probably be alarmed if they learned that MAR-A was going to be traveling on the same ship. Not that there was any actual reason for concern. MAR-A didn't randomly attack people. Didn't, despite certain behaviors that suggested otherwise, want to hurt anyone. Though its plasma guns and other offensive systems remained intact, MAR-A knew and despised the history of combat droids like it. Except when MAR-A *wanted* to scare someone. That was something MAR-A seemed to enjoy.

A recognition alert appeared in Jules view. It highlighted a woman walking into the waiting area, identifying her as Bri. He dismissed the alert, annoyed with it even though he had set the system to alert him. He would have noticed her without the alert.

As she entered the waiting area she was looking around, obviously searching for him. He lifted his head higher so that his face was more visible beneath the hood.

Bri met his eyes, and she didn't flinch this time. She smiled instead. He appreciated that. Even with all of the diverse species and droids around, some people struggled with a face that looked both human and artificial at the same time.

She started through the waiting passengers in his direction.

From the corner of the area, Jules noticed MAR-A moving silently forward. Bri hadn't seen the tall combat droid, her attention was on him.

Silently, Jules sent a text to MAR-A. "Don't try to scare her."

The droid halted in place. "I wasn't going to."

"Good." Jules sent. He stood up to greet Bri as she reached him.

"Bri, good morning."

"Thank you so much for agreeing to come take a look at our ship," Bri said.

He nodded. "Of course. We're glad to help."

"That's right," she said. "You said that you have a partner that is coming along to help?"

"I do." Jules gestured at MAR-A, now stalking through the waiting area. People flinched back as he passed them.

"This is MAR-A, an associate that has helped me in other cases."

Bri's breath caught as MAR-A reached them, skeletal face peering down at her from beneath the cowl.

"I scared you," MAR-A said in a tone that hinted at glee. "Briana Makkar."

Bri took a breath and let it out with a short laugh. "Sorry. It's silly, I know."

"It isn't silly," MAR-A said, voice grave.

Bri's eyes widened.

"What would be silly is *not* being scared when a combat unit of my ability approaches." MAR-A's gaze shifted to look at Jules. "Some people are less sensible."

"And some like to be intimidating for no good reason," Jules said. He focused on Bri. "MAR-A's tech allows it to help identify all sorts of issues with systems. Its sense of humor is unfortunate."

MAR-A made a hiss like a pressure valve release. "Only for those unable to appreciate it."

Bri looked between them as if she couldn't believe the interplay. "A combat droid and a medium, working together?"

In a voice like a cold wind rasping across dead bones, MAR-A said, "We both deal in death."

Jules rolled his eyes. "Except you don't go around hunting people."

MAR-A stared at him, eyes glinting beneath his cowl, scarlet light pulsing around the rims. Jules matched MAR-A's gaze and held it. He reached for that place of stillness and relaxed into it. With the living he sometimes could get glimpses of the person beneath the surface, their aura of energy. It wasn't what he felt with MAR-A. There was an aura but it had the color and texture of fog and cobwebs. It twisted in cold lines sticking to the combat droid, oozing across MAR-A's structure. At least some of the death MAR-A had dealt clung to it like a stink that the droid couldn't shake.

MAR-A made a bone-rattling sound and jerked back from Jules's gaze, taking a step back and turning its hooded face away.

"What just happened?" Bri said, looking between them.

Jules pulled his awareness back, blinked, and focused on her. "Nothing."

Bri didn't look convinced, but MAR-A remained turned half away. A fact that caused several other waiting passengers to move further away to other seats.

He moved to take a seat himself and Bri joined him. "Were you able to reach your ship and tell them we're coming?"

Bri nodded. "Teegan and the girls were very relieved to hear it. She tried to downplay it, but it sounds like things have been hard." She looked at her hands in her lap. "I hated leaving them."

MAR-A's head swung around to look at her. "Why did you leave them? Why not bring them with you?"

"We couldn't leave the ship without anyone on board. It might be a target for pirates. Or systems could break down."

Jules didn't think it that likely that pirates would be a problem, even if a comet farming ship was seen as a target. He supposed pirates might, if they detected the *Olympia*, raid it for consumables. It'd be a risk without much profit.

"If it is haunted, it might be necessary to abandon the ship," MAR-A said.

Bri looked alarmed. "We can't. Everything we own is in our ship. And its our home. We're not giving it up."

MAR-A shrugged. "You might die. Or worse."

"That's unlikely," Jules said. "We haven't confirmed it is haunted. And even if it is, there are things we can do."

He pulled back his hood, letting Bri see the beads in his hair. His prosthetic face normally drew enough attention that he didn't need more interest in the beads he wore.

Bri had done her research. She leaned slightly closer to look. Her hand twitched as if she wanted to touch them. "Those are all spirit beads?"

It would be harmless for her to touch them, but Jules didn't invite her to. "Yes. When it is necessary, I can confine a spirit to a container."

"What are they made of?"

MAR-A answered before Jules could. "Bone. Carved, shaped, and imbued to contain the spiritual energy."

"Bone?" Bri looked from the Jules to the droid and back.

"Yes." Jules didn't want to talk about that. Not now. It was premature. "Most spiritual beings don't interact with the material plane. They have their own ecosystems and habitats that have nothing to do with us. In rare cases, if it becomes necessary, we can trap an entity in a vessel that can contain the spiritual being, allowing it to be removed."

"Why wear them?" Bri said, asking the question that everyone asked.

Jules sent a quick text to MAR-A. "The vessel needs a connection. Wearing them makes it easy to maintain that connection without risk."

MAR-A cackled. "If he left them too long, something could get out."

Bri said, "What if something happens to you?"

"If he died?" MAR-A said with dry glee.

Bri kept looking at Jules. "Yes."

Jules shrugged. "The containment would hold for a time. MAR-A knows who to contact, or what to do if another medium can't get there in time."

Bri glanced up at MAR-A. "You've been working together for a long time?"

MAR-A's voice cracked like branches breaking. "Only as humans think. Not so long."

"MAR-A was trained by the medium that trained me," Jules said. "For a droid, not that long ago."

The droid loomed over them. "Humans don't live long."

Bri shivered, probably due to MAR-A's threatening tone. Jules smiled for her, not sure if *his* smile was any more reassuring than MAR-A's voice. "Don't let it get to you. MAR-A is exactly who we want with us."

Bri smiled like a candle flickering. "Okay. I think I'm going to rest, until boarding?"

"Good idea," Jules said. "I'll meditate."

"I'll keep watch," MAR-A said, turning to scan the waiting area.

Bri curled up on her side on the bench seat. Jules closed his eyes and watched his breath flow in and out. He opened himself to contemplate the flow of energy around them. He saw shapes like shadows in the fog moving through the waiting area. Wisps of figures half-seen and gone. None with the intensity to interact with the material plane.

In that other sense, the waiting area existed, along with the station and the ships. It was all an oasis in space. A spiritual ecosystem supported by all the various people inhabiting or passing through the station. In his other sight, the seats and structures looked much the same.

MAR-A's cowled shape dripped with glowing cobwebs of energy and fragments of spiritual beings clinging to the droid's structure.

Bri and the other living people in the area glowed with a candle-like light that illuminated their auras as they waited. *Life*. It burned in each of them. Some of the shadow shapes followed and circled the living. Or waited, letting the living pass through them and leave the tiniest fraction of energy. It wasn't dangerous. Not this sort of activity.

He watched his breath flow in and out and allowed the vision of that other place fade from his awareness. He watched from a distance as thoughts and emotions moved into view. As each appeared, he noted it, identified it as thought or emotion, and let it go.

Chapter 6

THE TRIP TO THE *Olympia* took three days but until the final morning on the transport ship, Bri hadn't told them anything about the events on her ship. Jules had hardly seen either MAR-A or Bri, since he mostly stayed in his cabin. Something MAR-A didn't do except for those times that Jules woke to find MAR-A lurking in the darker shadows of the cabin. Or when he got out of the shower and faced MAR-A's cavernous, "I scared you."

Each time, Jules looked at the droid without trying to hide anything. MAR-A's sensors could pick up on all of his biometric readings, heart rate, temperature, pupil dilation, respiration rate, and blood oxygen without even making contact. Each time MAR-A hissed or groaned with evident irritation and stomped off.

Probably observing passengers. Another favorite pastime of the combat droid.

On their final morning of the trip, Bri joined him in the dining hall for breakfast.

"Good morning," she said, as she reached his table.

Jules nodded. "Bri." He gestured to one of the empty chairs at the table. "Join me."

She smiled brightly, but he thought there was a bit of hesitation to it. *Rethinking this plan?*

She took the chair across from him, setting down a plate with a couple spongy-looking green wafers that smelled of honey and a cup of what was obviously coffee.

"Thank you," she said. "I called Tee this morning, got through this time."

"You've had trouble?"

"Around the gas giant," she said. "Too much interference. But they're okay, hanging in there."

Jules had already finished most of his breakfast. He picked up his last bacon strip (plant-based) and took a bite. It crunched between his teeth. Bri watched him eating, her fingers turning her coffee cup.

She lifted it, took a sip, and looked around the dining room. "MAR-A?"

"No idea," he said. "MAR-A does what they want."

He considered and rejected in the same instant the idea of sending a text to MAR-A. It was obvious that Bri had something on her mind. Whatever she wanted to tell him, he could record and share with MAR-A later—if he decided it was necessary.

Bri took another swallow and put the cup down. "I've been so worried. I couldn't even think about what might be happening. I felt guilty that I left them on the ship. I wondered if we were doing the right thing, maybe we should leave and try to start over."

"It's hard to start over with nothing," Jules said.

"Yeah," Bri said. "That's what I kept coming back to. We could have come to the station. Sold the *Olympia,* if we could find a buyer, but that doesn't seem likely."

"Why not?"

"She's a salvaged ship," Bri said. "With a reputation in the Station Association already. We didn't think there was anything to it."

He picked up a piece of cold toast and bit off the corner. Bri didn't flinch anymore when she looked at him, that was a nice change. It made him almost feel normal.

She sighed. "We wanted something different for our daughters than a stationer's life. A comet harvester ship, that's freedom. Independence."

"Teegan feels the same way?"

Bri laughed. "Oh yes. Tee loves the ship. She's not about to let go of it."

It felt like they were coming to what Bri wanted to tell him. He stayed silent as she took another drink of her coffee.

She met his gaze. "I should tell you what's been happening, right?"

He nodded. "If you want. You don't have to."

Sometimes people didn't want to say anything, suspicious that he was running a scam. He didn't think that was the case here. More likely that Bri was simply scared and didn't want to relive what had happened on the ship.

She took a breath. "I do. I think it's only fair that you know before we reach the ship. If you change your mind, you can still take the transport ship back to the station. It wouldn't be right to wait until it was gone."

"Okay," he said. He reached across the table and touched her wrist. "Tell me what happened. Why are you all scared?"

"I don't know what it, what they, want," Bri said. "I'm terrified about that."

Chapter 7

B RI OBVIOUSLY STEADIED HERSELF before she continued talking. Jules's heads-up picked up the obvious increase in the pulse visible in her neck.

"It's okay," he said. "We're here to help. How did you find out about the ship?"

Bri nodded. She took a breath and told her story.

We dreamed about owning our own ship. Instead of working for someone else, you know? Our chance to create our own homestead and legacy for our daughters.

I'm a genetic engineer, working mostly on pharmaceuticals. I enjoy the work, but the company controls the patents, receives most of the profits, and exploits people. I wanted to launch a startup and create original designs that could benefit people. If I did most of the work, contracted out the studies and trials, then I could afford to sell medicines at a reasonable price.

Teegan loves everything about spaceships. She knows it all. She's an engineer. Between us, we figured we could handle an ship with sufficient automation without needing additional crew at the start. And our girls, they're bright young women. They could already help with things.

We saved everything we could and made our plans. When the *Olympia* showed up at auction, it fit all of our criteria. A comet ship with its own environmental pods, resource extraction and storage pods, and it only required a minimal crew for the work we would be doing at the start. It'd been found adrift by a salvage crew, but everything was operational according to the reports. Teegan reviewed everything provided before we made the decision to bid. It'd take everything to get the ship and the essential equipment I needed to begin my work. I couldn't sleep after we placed the bid.

When celebrated when we won. Two months later, the transport ship we hired matched orbits with the *Olympia.*

It's a wheel-shaped craft with a wide inner ring and an outer ring not that much farther out. Each ring is made up of pods racked together in the framework. It's a flexible design because the pods can be raised and moved along the rings and reinserted. Or even ejected from the ship to send a pod to a new destination. Each is self-contained, but can link up. It makes it extremely flexible.

It wasn't the most welcoming sight from the transport ship. It was adrift. No running lights. The only light came from the salvage company's marker buoy, blinking near the inner ring. The transport picked up its signal, had been using it to approach the *Olympia*. Other than the light on the buoy, the only lights came from the dim sunlight and starlight. Most of the ship was in shadows and darkness, only the dull gleam of the exteriors of the pods caught the light. And the comet it still held. Even the solar sails were folded away.

Tee whistled when she saw it. "Okay. That looks cold and inactive. We can't just transfer over."

"What do you mean?" I said. "We have to. The transport won't stay."

Tee shook her head. "We can't go over if there's no environmental systems running. I like breathing. I need at least a couple days to make sure we're not going to suffocate, starve, or explosively decompress."

"I guess I'll talk to the transport company," I said, knowing this was going to be another draw on the few resources we had left. We were supposed to disembark ourselves and our cargo within six hours. That wasn't going to be enough time.

Even though it was at the end of their orbit, the transport company would be picking up additional passengers on the orbit back down the system's gravity well to the station. They agreed to adjusting their scheduled burns and charged us a premium for the day they gave us.

It wasn't a good sign, the ship adrift like that, but there wasn't anything we could do except try to get some part of it habitable in the limited time we had. Either that, or we'd have to go back and the transport costs, storage costs, and the rest would probably bankrupt us.

I don't know how she managed, but Tee didn't stop that whole day. She wouldn't let me help. Said it was too much of a risk, if something happened to us both, she didn't want our daughters orphaned. She made do with the ship's repair bots.

Every two hours she sent me a text saying, "Still working."

Later on she admitted she programmed it to be automatically sent so she didn't have to take the time to do it.

But before the day was up, she had several key pods up and working, the ship's orientation and spin stabilized, and confirmed there was enough resources in the storage pods to support us. She couldn't stop working—we still had to transfer over all of our cargo. I handled that end of it and was exhausted by the time we finished. She managed to unload everything onto the *Olympia* herself using the repair bots on semi-automatic. She hadn't had time to set up the system feed yet and didn't trust them.

In literally the last hour remaining, I transferred over with our daughters and personal items. When we put boots on the *Olympia's* decks the transport ship executed their burn and left. We still didn't have a functional drive. Most systems were offline. The environmental systems were operating at reduced capacity, only enough to keep the pods Tee had worked on survivable.

Our breath frosted in air that smelled of something like dry rot. Mel, our youngest, wrinkled her noise when I lifted off her helmet. "Pew. It stinks."

Sara, she is thirteen, removed her own helmet. She inhaled deeply and sighed. "Get used to it squirt, that's the smell of *our future.*"

"Got that right, kiddo," Tee said. She looked like death—(Bri glanced up at MAR-A and grimaced)—she had sunken cheeks, bruised eyes, and chapped lips. Her hair is blond, usually in short spikes, but it was plastered to her scalp like it had been dumped on her head.

"That's the smell of space-dried hydroponics exposed to air again for the first time in who knows how long. And you're going to be cleaning them all and setting them up or pretty soon we're not going to have food, clean water, *or* clean air."

"Of course," Sara said.

"I'll help," Mel said in her bright voice. Anything to spend time with her sister.

Tee pulled me aside while the girls squabble over who got which cabin in the habitation pod that Tee had brought online. She smelled of sweat and, I realized when I got close, blood. She had a gash on the back of her neck, covered by a bandage.

I reached out to her, to look, but she shrugged my hand off. "It's a scratch. Look, keep the girls in this pod or the hydroponics pod." She pointed out the hatch across the communal living area. "This place is big and I've barely had a chance to see any of it. Storage is through that other hatch, I've code locked it to our biometrics, but I don't want you going in there either. I'm going to get some sleep. If *anything* happens, wake me. Don't try to handle it. I have this place holding together with string and spit right now."

It scared me. She was so intense about it. I told her to get sleep. We'd be fine. She turned, leaving, but I caught her hand. It was cold and clammy. I smiled anyway and pulled her back for a kiss. She pulled back quickly.

"I stink worse than the ship. I'll sponge off before I go to sleep."

"I could help you," I said.

She shook her head. "Deal with those two. If I don't get up, wake me in six hours."

"You need more rest than that."

"Can't," she said. She gave me a look then that said things were much worse than I knew.

MAR-A stirred and leaned closer, making a sound like a dying gasp. "How much worse?"

She looked down at her cup, and for several long seconds, Jules wasn't sure she'd answer. Then she looked up and continued.

Worse. The salvage crew hadn't inspected the ship as thoroughly as they claimed. Tee said they didn't even put boots on the decks. Remote access only, to the few systems they could reach. For all they knew, there could have been crew still on the ship trying to hang on, unable to communicate, but with the power and systems down, they knew no one would be alive by the time they filed the salvage claim. The ship would get sold, they'd get their cut, and no risk.

Jules interlaced his fingers, disturbed by what Bri described. *If some of the crew was alive, and the salvage crew could rescue them?* But then they wouldn't be able to file a salvage claim.

"You found bodies," MAR-A said, voice quick and eager.

Bri shook her head. "No, not a single one."

Tee was afraid of that. She thought we might. It was part of the reason, other than the risks, that she didn't want anyone else exploring until she managed to clear all of the pods.

There were plenty of things left behind by the previous crew. The system had lost records–Teegan said she couldn't tell if the salvage ship had wiped the records or if the ship had suffered from a solar flare or something that had wiped the records. She said there might be other records in a secure storage, but hadn't had time to check. Since other systems remained intact for ship operations, she suspected the salvage crew used the feed to wipe systems. If there'd been any evidence they had actually come aboard, she might have thought they got rid of the crew, but she couldn't find any evidence. No logs or recordings. No physical trace disturbing the environment. The *Olympia* had recordings of the encounter with the salvage ship and those showed nothing left the salvager's ship. She couldn't be a hundred percent sure and it has bothered her ever since.

But we stayed. By that point, we didn't have any choice. We had to get the ship working and safe for our family. We couldn't leave. Sometimes we speculated about what happened to the previous crew, they left enough personal items that we knew who they were, but mostly we tried not to think about it. We sent an inventory of personal items and what we discovered to the station, put the items into a storage pod, and went back to the business of surviving and starting our future.

Bri lifted her cup and stopped, frowning at it. "I could use more coffee."

"Sure." Jules held out his hand. She hesitated as second, then gave it to him. He stood up to get the coffee. And something with *bounce* for himself.

She still hadn't gotten to the reason she came looking for him. The story was already disturbing enough.

Jules shivered, thinking about the ship they were flying toward.

Chapter 8

K NOWING THAT THE CREW had disappeared, I don't think any of us got much sleep the first week at least. Tee, especially, still trying to get systems to the point where she could rest without worrying that the air circulation wasn't going to fail and suffocate us in our sleep. Or the temperature control that might fail to keep the ship above absolute zero. Or prevent airlock failure so we didn't all explosively decompress. The girls did help by cleaning out all of the dead vegetation in the hydroponics pod. They purged the contaminated substrate. They couldn't do much after that, not until Tee had the water working.

If that wasn't enough, we kept hearing noises when we tried to sleep. Ever sleep in an unfamiliar place? You hear things and wonder if it is a bulkhead expanding or contracting, a fan unbalanced, or a short somewhere causing a noise. It was distracting, but I didn't think anything about it until the tenth night on the *Olympia*.

Tee was actually sleeping for once. The girls were in their cabin–instead of fighting over who got which cabin, they had decided to share. Surprised us, but we understood that it was a new ship and scary.

I couldn't sleep. My back ached from cleaning, moving supplies, doing a thousand different chores, and sorting and inspecting the equipment we had brought. Tee needed to get the ship operational, but then I needed to set up the lab pod, the experimental pods, control pods, design a plan, and start implementing it. My brain wouldn't shut off.

"Medications can do that," MAR-A said, raspy voice tinged with what sounded like glee.

Bri shook her head. "I try to avoid those."

"Why?" MAR-A's voice crackled with electricity. "You plan to create pharmaceuticals, why not use them?"

It was a fair question and Jules watched her. Bri didn't look embarrassed.

"If it was medically necessary, sure. This wasn't to that point. I was just awake thinking about the things I wanted to do, and in the back of my mind, listening to the noises."

It took me a second before I realized I'd heard a hatch open and close. I told myself that I'd imagined it. Everyone was asleep. Unless it was a utility bot, but tee didn't like scheduling them when we were trying to sleep.

I listened, not a hundred percent sure I'd heard it at all. Then I heard the footsteps.

It sounded like boots in the corridor outside. Heavy steps, unmistakable, slow, like someone tired—or someone in a spacesuit. Those aren't exactly meant for stealth.

I slid out of bed. Tee hadn't stirred. "Tee?"

She didn't respond. The footsteps hadn't stopped. They were coming around the corridor toward our room. That corridor makes a circle around the inner shaft of the pod and provides access to the rooms on that deck. It was getting closer, but the girls room was between our room and theirs.

"Tee!" I yelled, but as soon as I thought about the footsteps getting close to the girls I was already running.

I slammed through the hatch out into the corridor. The lights were dim to conserve power, the panels faintly illuminating the empty corridor as it curved away.

I ran ahead, thinking whoever it was must be running away and I didn't see anything. I stopped outside the girl's cabin and touched the panel. The hatch slid open. I could just make out their dark shapes in their bunks. Their breathing was soft and undisturbed.

I shut the hatch and locked it to prevent entry. The girls could still get out if they needed to, but it would slow down anyone trying to get to them.

Then I retreated back to our cabin and looked in. Tee hadn't gotten up at my shout. She had rolled over and was snoring. It was only then that I realized I'd run out into the corridor naked. It hadn't even occurred to me, I'd been so scared about the intruder. Who hadn't made a sound since I burst out of our cabin like a mad woman.

It seemed impossible that it could have been a dream. I was awake. I *heard* those footsteps. Maybe I was wrong that it was on this level. The sound could have traveled from another level. Thinking that there could still be an intruder, I stepped into our cabin and dressed quickly. I took one of the emergency flashes with me and went out hunting.

Each pod on the *Olympia* is essentially its own unit. They start out the same, a pill-shaped unit flattened on the bottom and top, equipped with locks and hookups so pods can be joined together. Each with its own environmental system, linking the pods improves efficiency but the redundancy means pods can be isolated in an emergency. Other than key systems, each pod can be configured and set up with modular decks, bulkheads, hatches, and other systems to create whatever sort of space is needed. Since the *Olympia* is a comet harvester ship, it also carries storage and refinement pods used to process cometary material.

Bri smiled, shaking her head. "Sorry. That's not what you want to hear."

"No," MAR-A said. "It isn't. Tell us about the intruder."

Jules didn't say anything. He met Bri's gaze and gave her a nod, already understanding what she was going to say.

I didn't find anything. I spent an hour going through the pod deck-by-deck. We were *alone*. I confirmed none of the locks had been opened. The ship's systems didn't show any spacecraft nearby. All of our suits were secure in their lockers. Nothing seemed out of place.

By the time I gave up, exhausted, I convinced myself that I had imagined the footsteps outside our rooms. There wasn't any other explanation. I had thought I was awake, but I must have been asleep having a false awakening dream. Or, if I wasn't asleep, I was so tired that my mind was just playing tricks on me. I went back to our cabin–Tee still hadn't waked and it was hours yet until morning– undressed, and got back into bed. I was asleep almost immediately.

I told Tee over breakfast, laughing it off as a weird dream. By then it felt like a dream. Tee was annoyed, thinking I was scaring the girls. I reassured them it was only a silly dream, being in a new place, and that we didn't have anything to be afraid of.

That night Mel and Sara came to our cabin. Tee woke up first, shook me away. The first thing I thought about was the footsteps in the corridor and right then it didn't seem quite as impossible.

But it was only the girls, silhouetted in the open hatch.

"What's wrong, sweet girls?" Tee said, beckoning to them.

They came into the cabin and Mel ran over to jump on our bunk. "It stinks in our cabin."

"Stinks?" I said, sleepy and not following.

Sara said, "She's right. It smells like something *rotten* in there. It's really gross."

Tee smiled like she wanted to tear out someone's throat. "Wonderfuck. These systems."

She slid out of the bunk, pulled her workall up over her thin frame. I noticed her ribs stood out, and she had a dark bruise on one hip–probably from climbing through access hatches to work on systems. She got her boots on, laced them up.

"Do you want help?" I said.

Tee shook her head. "No. Girls, why don't you get into the bunk with Mama Bri? I'll check it out and call if I need anything."

They got into the bunk. Sarah fell asleep in the middle right away. Mel looked like she wasn't going to go to sleep. I couldn't sleep either, trying to think of all of the things that could possibly go wrong to cause the smell in the girls' cabin. We couldn't smell anything in our cabin, which seemed weird to me. They're all on the same system.

My node buzzed. I checked my feed and found a message from Tee.

"Come here."

I whispered to Mel. "Mama Tee wants me. Stay here, I'll be back soon."

Mel scrunched down in the blankets, nodded, and rolled over to cuddle with Sarah.

I got up, pulled on my own workall, left my shoes and went barefoot out of the cabin and down to the girls' cabin. The hatch was open, lights on full.

I walked in. Tee was waiting in the middle of the room. She looked at me expectantly but didn't say anything.

I looked back. "What?"

"What do you smell?"

I got her point. I inhaled. The air, fresher thanks to Tee's work, smelled fine. I didn't smell anything bad.

"You fixed it," I said, reaching for her hands.

Tee crossed her arms and shook her head. "I didn't do anything. I couldn't smell anything." She pulled a tablet from her pocket. "Nothing is showing out of line as far as the sensors can detect. An odor is composed of *something*. There has to be molecules or gasses for our odor receptors to detect. Our nose is more sensitive when it comes to odors than the system, but I've got nothing. I hoped you might pick something up I missed."

Then I got what she was saying. It wasn't like the girls to make up a story like this. I closed my eyes and inhaled deeply, trying to focus on what I smelled.

Our sweat, mine and Tee's, faint, but there. The fresh, dry smell of the air in the room. Maybe too dry, Tee was still adjusting the humidity levels. The girls' mingled scents were there, a faint background odor marking the space. I didn't smell anything out of place.

I opened my eyes, shaking my head. "I don't smell anything unusual."

An announcement interrupted Bri. They had one hour until their arrival at the *Olympia.*

The things that she had described so far, the sound of footsteps in the corridor, the odor in the girls' room, both could be signs of something–or nothing more than they seemed. Imagination, a story told by kids, the inconsequential and unexplained things that might happen on an isolated and salvaged ship.

Jules said, "You didn't come all this way looking for help because of those incidents."

Bri's eyes were bright, tears threatening to spill. "No. Not because of that."

Chapter 9

MAR-A HISSED LIKE AN angry cat. Bri jerked in surprise and Jules glared at the tall combat droid.

"What are you doing?" Jules said.

MAR-A lifted an arm, bony finger uncurling to point at Bri. "She delays. We should have heard all of this before we left."

Bri lowered her head, not looking at either of them.

Jules said, "I came knowing that it might turn out to be nothing supernatural going on. No one twisted your arm about coming. You jumped at the chance."

MAR-A pulled back, folding arms into its robes.

Jules leaned forward, his arms on the table. "Bri, please. It would be good to know what's happened already before we arrive."

Bri looked up at him, eyes bright, but her mouth set. She said, "I know. I'm just not sure you'll believe me."

Interesting. He was a medium, after all. "Why is that?"

Bri shrugged. "We did our research. What's been happening, it's not exactly the norm."

"Each situation is unique," Jules said. He gestured at the beads in his hair. "I know that better than most."

She glanced up at MAR-, then back to him. "Okay. I've told you how it started. I'll tell you why I came to find you."

If it'd only been the odor in the girl's room or me hearing footsteps in the corridor, if it stopped with that, we could have dismissed it. Cases of nerves in a strange new place.

It didn't stop there.

The foul odor came and went in the girls' cabin, so they moved to a cabin on the other side of ours. Tee sealed the door on the other, but we'd find it open again. We had footage of it opening with no one there. Drove Tee crazy. At one point, I think she suspected that Sara had hacked the door controls as a prank.

The problems seemed to multiply as Tee brought more pods online, and we started preparing for the experiments.

I needed lots of growing medium for the pharmaceutical plants I wanted to test. The *Olympia* has plenty of pods, but each needed to be inspected, configured, and tested before it can be used. Tee was working around the clock. The ship is on an established orbit, automated, so it wasn't like we needed to pilot the ship.

The disturbances increased. We heard footsteps. Sometimes what sounded like people talking. Hatches and doors opening or closing on their own. For a while, Tee still thought that it had to be the system. Some problem in the code, though she couldn't find it.

Then whatever was going on targeted Mel. Our sweet little girl.

We first learned of it when Sara burst into our room one night, frantic and scared.

"I can't find her," Sara said.

I sat up. Tee lifted her head. I said, "Mel?"

Sara nodded. "She isn't in her bunk!"

"Lav?" Tee said, sleepily.

Sara shook her head. "No, Mama Tee. I checked. And the common area. She's scared of the dark. I don't know where she could have gone."

I was out of our bunk before she finished speaking, pulling on my discarded workall. I shoved my feet into my boots and stood.

Tee'd sat up and was sliding out of bed. She waved a hand. "Go, I'm coming."

I nodded to Sara and led the way out of our cabin. I went to their cabin first, Sara on my heels.

"She's not in here," Sara complained.

"Making sure she didn't come back," I said. A quick sweep of the cabin made it clear that Mel wasn't in there.

I went back out, back past our cabin where Tee was nearly dressed, and on to the girl's old cabin. I opened the door and went in convinced I'd find Mel in her old bunk.

The room was empty. I was scared before, but in those few seconds I'd concocted the explanation that Mel had gone to the lav, and sleepy, went back to the wrong cabin. My heart rate accelerated and I fought against the fear.

I didn't say anything to Sara. I left the cabin and went on down to the lav, knowing that she'd already checked, but unable to do anything except double-check.

No Mel.

Tee met us in the corridor. She pointed back down the other way. "I'll go this way, you go that. Check all the cabins."

"Keep calling her name," I said.

We all hurried on, calling out Mel's name as we went.

She wasn't in any of the cabins in the pod.

Not the common area, kitchen, utility room, or my temporary offices.

I thought about the footsteps I'd heard. What if there was someone still on the *Olympia?* Hiding from us, and they'd taken her?

I was heading out into the outer sections of the pod, screaming her name by that point, before I heard a faint thumping noise. It was hard to hear. I had to stop calling out to follow it at first. Until I reached the passage to the primary airlock. Then I *knew.*

I ran to the lock. The inner hatch was closed. I looked through the window and there Mel was, inside the lock, trying to walk forward, and each time her head bumped into the outer hatch.

I pounded on the hatch and called her name. She didn't respond. I jumped to the controls and saw that the cycle had started, the lock was depressurizing. It took me two tries to cancel and reverse the cycle. The whole time, she kept walking into the hatch.

My node buzzed while I waited for the hatch to open. It was Tee. I answered.

"She's in the airlock," I said. "It was cycling, but I've reversed it. I'll have her out in–"

"Bri–she's here with me now!"

I froze. I couldn't understand what she was saying. The *thumping* in the lock continued.

Then on the phone, Mel said, "I'm here, Mama Bri!"

I threw myself at the hatch window. Mel wasn't in the airlock. The outer hatch was open. It moved, jerked to a stop, and pulled back again like it was jammed. *That's* what made the thumping noise.

I couldn't breathe, I was so scared. In the phone Mel said, "Mama Bri–"

"Bri," Tee said, cutting her off. "Don't open the airlock. Do you hear me? Bri!"

It took me a second to reach the controls. What I saw didn't make sense. The outer airlock door continued thumping, but now the system was pouring atmosphere uselessly into the lock because of the commands I'd entered. The ship was venting. Eventually that would mean we'd suffocate, but worse was the countdown for the emergency airlock override that would force the inner hatch open.

Only seconds remained.

I hit the emergency stop–shutting the airlock down completely and taking it offline.

"Bri? Bri? Are you there?" Tee's voice came from the phone.

I slumped down to the floor with my knees drawn up. I wrapped my arms around them and clutched the phone.

"I stopped it," I said. "Shut down the airlock."

Tee didn't answer on the phone because she came at a run down the passage with both girls running behind her.

Seeing Mel, I gave a cry and shoved myself off the deck. I caught her, dropped to my knees and held her close. Tee and Sara embraced us, and we all clung to each other.

MAR-A said, "You hallucinated the girl in the airlock."

Bri looked up at the combat droid. Her voice was hoarse with remembered emotion. "I didn't. Airlock cameras showed the apparition."

"Do you have it?" Jules said.

"Yes." Bri took out a small tablet, flipped through, then slid it across the table to him.

MAR-A bent over Jules as he picked up the phone. It showed a video, paused. A girl stood in front of an airlock door. Her face wasn't visible. She had long, straight brown hair. It couldn't have been wet, given the shine. The airlock looked unremarkable, standard, with light panels, circular floor vents, and tie-ons around the entrance.

Jules touched the screen and the video played.

The girl stepped forward, head leading, and *thumped* against the hatch. She repeated the behavior with the next step. The image quality wasn't as good as he'd expected. Both the girl and the airlock hatch appeared out of focus. They jerked in the video, jittering with each *thump*. There was an afterimage of the hatch open for an instant after she hit the hatch. Jules stopped it on that frame, pointing it out.

"There. The hatch looks open, but the next frame it's closed again."

"The images have been altered," MAR-A said.

Bri said, "It hasn't. I checked for tampering. There wasn't any. It's what I saw."

Jules let it play until the girl vanished. The hiss of air flooding the airlock was audible. The outer hatch was open nearly all the way. It advanced a few centimeters before *thumping* to a stop.

He rewound the video and turned it to face Bri. "Did you see this jittering?"

She nodded. "After, when we checked the video. I don't remember if I saw it when I looked in the airlock. I was so scared at the time, I didn't even recognize that the girl *wasn't* Mel."

MAR-A's metal face lifted. "Who is the girl?"

Bri shrugged. "I don't know. She's taller than Mel, with longer hair. Mel's barely reaches her shoulders, and is darker."

"You didn't realize that until looking at the video?" Jules said.

"Right," she said. "I was so scared and freaked out, it was hours until we thought to check the video. Tee went through it. The hatch opens on its own and then gets stuck. It thumps in place until the girl appears and then a *ghost hatch* hides the real one. Until they disappear When I shut down the lock."

Jules passed the phone back to Bri.

"Send me the video," MAR-A said.

Jules looked up at the droid, eyes narrowing.

MAR-A looked from him back to Bri. "Please."

Satisfied, Jules folded his hands. "That's what convinced you to come find us?"

"Yes," she said. "And other things. But we came so close to depressurizing the entire pod, we knew we needed help. And the other things, the disturbances were getting worse everyday. No one was sleeping."

"And since you've been gone?"

Bri shook her head. "I still haven't been able to sleep. I'm worried about them. Tee is holding it together, but I don't know how long she can do that."

"We're almost there," Jules said. "Why don't we all prepare for our arrival? I'd like to meditate before we get there."

"Okay," Bri said.

MAR-A remained silent and unmoving. Not wanting, Jules thought, to reveal anything unnecessarily to Bri.

She stood up and stepped back from the table. "Thank you both, again. It's a comfort knowing you'll be there to help us."

"Yes," MAR-A said.

"You'll be back with your family soon," Jules said. "We only have thirty minutes or so until we arrive."

"Twenty-six," MAR-A said.

"I can't wait," Bri said. "I'll see you when we get there."

She left and Jules stood up. He pushed in his chair and stood with his hands on its back.

MAR-A drifted closer. "Spirits usually lack malevolent intent. What is this?"

That was the question Jules had been avoiding since he saw the video. It looked as if the entity wanted Bri to open the airlock.

"I don't know," he said, looking at the droid. "If it opened the outer door, why couldn't it open the inner door and depressurize the pod if that was the goal?"

"The outer hatch is normally unsecured," MAR-A said. "To allow ease of entry in case of emergencies. But the inner hatch may require codes to open."

Jules nodded. MAR-A made a good point. "So it could trigger the outer hatch to open, make it jam, but couldn't open the inner hatch without someone entering the codes to do so."

"It nearly succeeded," MAR-A said. His hands rose. "It *scared* her. It *scared* you, watching the video."

And that was also the truth.

Chapter 10

JULES WATCHED THEIR APPROACH from the passenger's observation lounge. With the *Olympia* as the transport's apogee stop, he had the lounge to himself. The room's outer wall was a large curved window some six meters high that ran the length of cylindrical room. At the back of the room were risers with adjustable seats designed to accommodate a variety of species, the color of the entire room a matte dark gray, like the color of an asteroid's surface. The seats and the flat area of floor that ran out to the window had the same pebbled texture.

He stood at rest, hands clasped behind his back. His hood was down as he gazed up at the comet harvester ship. The window's transparent and non-reflective surface made it seem as if he was standing in open space beneath the window curving overhead.

And out there, large and growing larger, was the wheel shape of the *Olympia* with the pods arrayed around the perimeter. They were approaching the ship almost edge-on at this point. The transport itself wouldn't dock with the ship. They would match the *Olympia*'s rotation and then use a transfer pod to cross the distance between the ships.

Jules had already sent his baggage bot on ahead to board the transfer pod. He had wanted to *see* the *Olympia* from outside before he went over to the ship.

The surface of the ship looked *old*. Pitting was visible across the surfaces. Comet harvester, even with the best containment, exposed the ship to lose particles and debris. Sharing the same orbit, those fragments could come back and impact the ship. He was surprised to see the curve of an icy comet clutched by the ship's arms within the central ring of the *Olympia*. From this angle it wasn't easy to see much of it, the ship blocked most of the view, but he could see the pits that the arms had carved out of the surface. It almost looked like the rough profile of a skull clutched by a metal spider.

Jules pushed aside the fanciful idea. *Not a skull,* just a rough-hewn comet being carved up by the ship.

At least it showed the *Olympia* was functional. It would carve up pieces of the comet, ingest them, and process and separate the resources for storage or use in the life-support systems.

Bri's story, backed by the video footage, was disturbing him. He didn't like what it suggested about what was happening on the ship. He wished he knew what had happened to the previous crew. If they had died, where did the bodies go? It didn't sound like the salvage crew had come aboard, so they wouldn't have removed the crew.

That was one question he wanted an answer to, but there were so many others.

The view continued to change as the transport matched the *Olympia's* orientation and rotation. The distance between the ships decreased as the transport moved closer, as if it was going to dock with the comet harvester.

As they came alongside the *Olympia*, he saw the band of the ship curving up and away on both sides. He looked up, seeing the captured comet from below, no trace of the skull he had imagined. Straight ahead, he faced the pods. With both ships matching rotation, the pods remained still outside.

"Boarding call," a voice said. "All passengers to the transfer pod for the *Olympia*. Boarding call for the *Olympia*."

This close, the pods looked worn, pitted, and darkened by time in space. The airlock hatch, a bright green color that contrasted with the graphite of the pod's surface, was closed. *That's where it happened.* Where they had captured footage of that spirit.

Jules turned from the view and walked out of the lounge. The Makkars needed his help.

Chapter 11

T HERE WAS NO ONE to see them off. The transport ship was largely automated and the crew maintained a separation from the passengers.

Bri was there, waiting, when Jules arrived. She smiled at him.

"Hey there," he said. He glanced around the small boarding area. "MAR-A?"

Bri shrugged. "I haven't seen it."

Jules sighed. "Then expect it to pop out and try to scare you."

Her eyes widened. "Why would it do that?"

"Your guess is as good as mine," he said. "I'm guessing psychological trauma."

A dark shape flowed up, joints cracking, from behind the boarding seats. MAR-A loomed up in front of them.

"Scared you." It paused, the said, "I have no trauma."

Jules exchanged a look with Bri. Then he gestured at the open hatch. "Shall we?"

MAR-A hissed like an angry cat, spun around, robes swirling around it, and stomped across the boarding area. The combat droid had to duck to get through the hatch.

Bri went next. Jules followed her. He stepped through the hatch without any hesitation. Actually eager, he realized. Not that he wasn't scared. Fear was a rational response to what Bri had shared. At the same time, he was eager. This was his calling, to help people. After all of the travel to get here, he wanted to get to work.

The transfer pod was a small, automated craft with seats for ten passengers. MAR-A sat hunched in the front seat on the right. Bri had taken the last seat on the left. Jules sat in the seat across the aisle from her. The pod's soft voice asked them to strap into the seats. Jules pulled the straps into place and fastened them.

A clang behind them was the hatch closing. A series of thumps as the clamps disengaged. The tiniest push and they were free of the transport. The pod lacked any views of what was happening. It didn't have any windows. Not that it mattered, Jules reasoned. The crossing between the ships wouldn't take long.

Five minutes. That's how long it took before they felt the answering thrust barely pushing them forward against their straps, and then the sound of docking vibrated through the ship. The pod had hatches on both ends, eliminating the need to rotate the craft during the crossing.

"Docking secure. Please retrieve your baggage and move forward to disembark."

Jules unstrapped and stood. "Baggage?"

A compartment behind the seats opened and the baggage bot rolled free. "Ready to go."

MAR-A's position at the front allowed the combat droid to go first, moving quickly to the hatch that hadn't opened yet. Bri carried her own bag and Jules motioned her forward.

"MAR-A," he called. "Come back here. Let Bri go first."

MAR-A twisted around. The lights around its eyes darkening. "Why?"

"Manners. It's her family. They should see her first."

Bri stood to one side beside the first seat that MAR-A had vacated. Her bag hung from a shoulder strap over her arm.

Clattering with displeasure, MAR-A moved away from the hatch. The droid came down the aisle, passed Bri without looking at her, and then stopped and stared at Jules.

"Thank you," Bri said to MAR-A's back and went down to the hatch.

Jules looked up at MAR-A. "Are you going to sulk, or follow her?"

MAR-A's head tilted. "You don't wish to go before me?"

Jules shook his head, knowing that MAR-A was trying to provoke an argument. "No reason to. You go ahead."

Soundless now, MAR-A spun about and sprang down the aisle as if in pursuit of Bri. Jules laid a hand on the back of the baggage bot. "Lead the way."

Obligingly, the baggage bot crawled ahead after MAR-A and Jules followed. With MAR-A in front of him, tall shape deliberately standing straighter than normal to fill the passage, Jules couldn't see the moment when the hatch opened, but he heard it.

There were the normal sounds of the hatch sliding open, the clank and hiss of air as it equalized, and then a chorus of ear-piercing squealing.

He grinned. That could only be Bri's daughters, happy to see "Mama Bri" return. There was more, Bri's voice and another woman—obviously Tee.

"Are they attacking?" MAR-A inquired.

Bri, laughing, said, "No. Just greeting."

MAR-A rocked forward, bending as it looked down. "I scared you?"

A sweet high voice answered. "No. What's your name? I'm Melanie, but everyone calls me Mel. That's Mama Teegan, but we call her Tee. And *that's* Sara. Just Sara. She doesn't like to be called Sar."

"I'm MAR-A," the droid said.

"Really?" Another girl said, sounding older.

"Like Sara?" Mel said suspiciously.

"That's correct," MAR-A said.

Jules heard Mel's huff, then she said, "Can I call you Mar?"

"If you wish," MAR-A said.

"You don't need to shorten everyone's name," Sara said, obviously talking to her sister.

Tee said, "Let's move out of the way girls, let them come aboard."

That got everyone moving. MAR-A followed Bri out of the transfer pod, the baggage bot trailed after, and finally Jules got to see the family they'd come to help.

Tee's lanky form and spiky blond hair was what he'd expected. Her hair looked wet. The light shirt and dark leggings clean, the lack of sleeves on the shirt showed the lean muscles in her arms, one around each of their girls.

Sara obviously took after Tee. Same build, her blond hair the same color but long and pulled back. She wore a clean workall, sleeves rolled up, front open to show a dark undershirt beneath.

On Tee's other side stood Mel, the younger girl. She resembled both her parents. Bright red hair like Bri, clearly a shorter child, with a galaxy of freckles across her cheeks and nose. Despite her height, she still was thin and lanky looking, as if Tee were scaled down. And it was Tee's pale eyes that looked curiously at him.

MAR-A had gone on down the passage from the airlock past the family. It stood there, arms folded. Bri faced her family across the passage, and gestured to Jules.

"This is Jules. Jules, everyone."

The baggage bot moved gracefully to the side out of his path as he walked toward them. He held out his hand to Mel first.

"I'm glad to meet you," he said.

Mel looked up at him with wide eyes, then at her mother. Tee nudged her. Sara rolled her eyes.

Mel extended her hand. He took her smaller hand in his and shook it.

"Glad to meet you," she said, barely above a whisper.

He smiled, released her hand, and turned to Sara. A flush rose in her cheeks, but she quickly thrust her hand at him. He shook her hand.

"Hi," she said.

"Hi." He smiled. He wanted to build trust with the family. It was going to be important.

"You're a medium?"

He nodded, releasing her hand. "Yes, I am."

Her eyes went from his face to his hair, her gaze focusing. "Those are spirit beads. I've read about them."

The fact that none of them showed any shock at his prosthetic face made it clear that Bri had prepared them. It was a nice change.

"That's right," he said.

His attention shifted to Tee. She accepted his hand, her grip hard, but not in challenge. "Thank you," she said. "We're so glad you agreed to help."

Both girls nodded enthusiastically.

Bri stepped up beside him. "Why don't we get you settled? You can rest before dinner."

He shook his head. "My body still thinks it is early. I'd like to get started once I show my baggage to my cabin."

"Sure," Tee said. "Sara? Will you show Jules his cabin?"

"Okay." Sara stepped away from Tee. "It's this way."

Mel darted away toward MAR-A, skidding to a stop to look up at the big droid. "I can show you your cabin."

"A cabin is unnecessary," MAR-A intoned. "I don't sleep."

Mel giggled. "I know that, silly. You're a droid! But that doesn't mean you shouldn't have a cabin too and we've got lots of them."

Before MAR-A had formulated another answer, Mel grabbed its hand and tugged it down the passage.

Bri was still standing beside Jules. "I hope that's okay?"

"It is," Jules said, trying to sound reassuring. "I wouldn't bring MAR-A if they weren't safe around kids. I think they enjoy kids more than adults."

"But it's a combat droid," Tee said.

"Yes," Jules said. "And the it uses its sophisticated sensors and technology to help me now with my investigations. I've found them invaluable–once you get past the personality quirks."

"It's kind of creepy," Sara said.

"They are," Jules said. "But harmless when it comes to humans, despite their origin."

Sara stood, shifting her weight, obviously impatient. Jules said, "Let's go."

He glanced at the two women. Tee nodded and moved closer to Bri, slipping her arm around Bri's waist.

"We'll be in the common area," Tee said, "when you're ready."

"I won't be long," he promised.

As he moved, Sara walked ahead. Her steps suggested that she'd rather run through the pod, but she was keeping herself to a walking pace. Jules lengthened his stride, catching up with her, and then making her walk faster to keep up.

She grinned at him.

The baggage bot crawled gamely after them.

Entering the common area, he found himself in a large space with a high ceiling. Furniture set up in the space were padded with dark, rust-colored cushions uncomfortably close to the color of dried blood. The couches and chairs themselves looked comfortable enough. Various hatches led out of the room. On one side was a dining area and an opening that had to lead to a kitchen. A bar with stools occupied one section of the wall—the space clearly designed for crew entertainment. Up above, hexagonal windows looked out from other levels into the space.

"This is the common area," Sara said.

Sara led him to a ramp that circled up around the pod to each level. "There are lifts," she pointed to the other side of the large room. "If you'd rather?"

Jules shook his head. "I like the exercise."

That earned him another grin.

Her pace slowed somewhat on the ramp. They walked beside each other. Sara's face grew more serious. His displays showed him her elevated heart rate and respiration. Nothing dangerous, but also not caused solely by the walk.

"I don't use the lifts anymore," Sara confided.

"No?"

She shook her head. "No."

He sensed there was more to it than that, but Sara didn't offer an explanation, and they reached the next level and came out into the corridor that curved around the central area of the pod. Here were the heaxgonal windows looked out into the central space. There were doors on the other side, widely spaced, that had to be the cabins.

Sara pointed to the next door on the right. "We set up this cabin for you."

Jules walked to it, Sara followed slightly behind with the baggage bot. A panel next to the door had the usual features, touch-screen that could be coded. He touched the panel, waking it and tapped the open button.

The door slid silently open and a dark shape stood there, towering over him. Sara yelped. Jules rolled his eyes as he looked up at MAR-A.

"Scared you," MAR-A said. Behind the combat droid, Mel started giggling.

Chapter 12

J ULES DIDN'T WASTE ANY time. Sara had escorted the protesting Mel back down to the common area. He surveyed the small cabin. Not bad, actually. Small seating area, inset bunk in the far wall, some built-in storage drawers and cupboards. A door opened into a bathroom complete with a large tub and a separate shower. Water wasn't in short supply on a comet harvester. There were a few touches courtesy the Makkars, clean towels and bedding, and most surprising, a small vase on the table in the corner holding three yellow flowers. He didn't know the name and didn't bother looking it up. Those must have been grown in the hydroponics.

As he surveyed the cabin, MAR-A stayed by the door, watching him. The baggage bot crouched in the corner as if it wanted to keep its distance from the large combat droid.

Jules crossed the room and addressed the baggage bot. "Unpack. Clothes in those drawers." He pointed. "When you're done, store yourself."

The baggage bot chirruped a cheerful tone and rose, scurrying off to do as instructed.

Jules turned and looked at MAR-A. "Are you ready to get to work?"

"Always ready," MAR-A said.

"Good. Ask Tee for access to the systems and feed. I want you to set up monitors throughout the ship."

"I could crack the system to gain access."

Jules shook his head. "Ask, okay? We're invited. You don't need to hack their systems. And *after* Tee gives you access, see what you can pull up about the previous crew. Maybe you can reconstruct something."

MAR-A nodded slowly.

Jules took a breath and let it out. So far he hadn't opened himself to *feel* anything from this place. A defensive reaction, and his habit. He kept his mental shields in place to protect himself. He had to open himself to the spiritual ecosystem on this ship if he was going to get to the bottom of what was going on.

"Let's go back down," Jules said.

They left the cabin, him leading. In the corridor outside he mentally relaxed and *looked* with his other sense. It was like turning on a flashlight in the dark, trying to see what was hidden around him.

Nothing caught his attention in the corridor. He pointed down the corridor, away from the ramp, then started walking that way. The corridor showed signs of care. The panels on the floor were polished, a dark bluish color with brighter specks that gleamed beneath the white light panels. It was tall enough that MAR-A didn't have to stoop. The inside wall had regularly space hexagonal windows that looked into the central well. They passed three cabins after going about a quarter of the way around the curve—so probably sixteen cabins in total on this level.

Moving through the space, he wasn't picking up any other presences. At least not right now. The lift doors were ahead on the left, interrupting the pattern of windows. MAR-A lengthened their stride and touched the panel to call the lift.

It arrived seconds later with a soft chime and the doors slid open. After Sara's comments about the lift, he half expected something to appear inside, but didn't see anything. MAR-A stomped into the lift.

Jules followed. There were doors on the other side too, with more of the hexagonal windows set into each side in a long zigzag pattern. He crossed to the windows as the doors slid shut behind him and the lift started down.

The Makkars were gathered in the common area below. Tee was behind the bar on one side of the room, Bri sitting on a stool in front of it. The girls were over on a long couch talking with a lot of gesturing and Mel laughing, clutching her stomach.

He shivered. There was a lot of excitement and happiness at being reunited with Bri, and in having guests.

But for the first time since he had *looked*, he got a sense of a presence as he looked at the family. It was almost as if a cloud had gathered around them. Not a cloud, fog. Something cold that drifted among and between them. It wasn't visible. Not in the way normal things were, but it showed in his sight.

The lift came to a stop. Outside the family all turned to look in their direction as the doors slid open. Jules smiled and walked out. MAR-A brushed past him and headed across the room toward Tee with long strides.

He suppressed a smile. MAR-A could be very literal.

He stopped in front of the couch where the girls sat. "Hi again."

Mel waved a hand at him. "Hi!"

Sara rolled her eyes.

"May I have access to your systems?" MAR-A said to Tee.

"Uh," Tee looked at Bri, then Jules.

He nodded.

"Sure," Tee said. "I'll send you a key."

"Thank you." MAR-A settled another bar stool and folded his arms in a contemplative posture.

"Can I get you something?" Tee asked, looking at Jules.

"Water would be nice."

Bri laughed. "We have plenty of that."

"I noticed the comet as we approached."

"It saved us time," Tee said. "It was already there when we arrived. I've been testing the the systems."

Tee brought a glass around the bar and crossed the room. Bri slid off the stool and followed. When she reached him, Tee extended the glass.

The glass was cold to the touch, water over ice. He sipped and gasped from the cold. It tasted pure in a way that station water never could. Scientists said there wasn't any difference, but water that had never passed though a living thing before instead of being recycled, had an ineffable quality.

Tee grinned. "It's pure crushed comet ice. It's a waste product of our processing since the system produces more water than we can use."

"It's good," Jules said. "Thank you."

Bri had settled on the couch between the girls, her arms around them, holding them close.

Tee crossed her arms. "How do you want to do this?"

He gestured for her to be seated, then took one of the chairs facing the couch. Tee perched on the arm of the couch.

The presence he sensed still drifted through the room like an invisible cold fog. It coiled around the family on the couch, tendrils stroking across them. He didn't watch it directly, looking past it at the people. It was vague. Impossible to tell yet if it had any hostile intent. Many spirits were perfectly content in the spiritual plane, only occasionally paying attention to the material plane.

"I'd like you to show me around," he said, looking directly at Tee. "This pod has been where most of the incidents have happened?"

"Yes," Tee said.

Mel turned around, going onto her knees and holding onto the back of the couch. She looked at MAR-A sitting like a statue at the bar. She looked down at Bri. "Is he okay?"

"It's fine," Bri said.

"Yes," Jules said. "MAR-A is having fun doing what they enjoy, looking through your systems and setting up monitors."

Mel turned back around, flopping down on the couch. "Monitors?"

"Alerts," Sara said, her tone impatient. "To tell them if anything happens."

"That's right," Jules said. "MAR-A will monitor the ship for movement, sudden temperature or pressure changes, or abnormal sounds."

"Like the girl in the airlock," Mel said, her tone becoming solemn.

Jules said, "Yes, like that. Or anything else that the instruments can pick up. Sometimes it doesn't work, but other times like that incident in the airlock it does."

"We're haunted," Tee said. "Do we just have to live with it?"

Jules shook his head. "I can't tell you that. Not yet, at least. It could be a haunting, but it could be something else."

"Something else?" Bri said.

"A non-human spirit. Something that was never alive. What people used to call a demon."

At the word, MAR-A's head turned soundlessly, eyes beneath his cowl looking at the other humans. Jules ignored the droid and focused on the family in front of him while keeping his other sense open.

Bri's eyes immediately looked wet, and she bit her bottom lip, pulling the girls tighter against her. Tee arched an eyebrow, but didn't comment. Both of the girls looked scared.

He spread his hands. "I'm not saying that's the case. I am getting a sense of a presence here. It isn't clear yet what it is, but in these situations I find it better to consider the worst case scenario until it proves to be something else."

Tee rubbed her hands on her knees. "Demon? That's the worst-case scenario?"

"Most likely," Jules said. "Spiritual or supernatural ecosystems were proven to exist almost two hundred years ago after centuries of superstitious and religious belief. It's what Butlerians call the reconciliation. What we think of as supernatural today refers to that other dimension. We're all connected to it during our lives and we have some form of continuation after we're dead. That part of us continues."

He looked at each of them. Scared, yes, but attentive and doing okay, all things considered.

"This other plane of existence is usually distant enough that we don't notice it. But there are places where it is much closer. We might see repeaters, spirits that repeat their final moments or moments from their life. There can be any number of entities. It's a challenge to investigate this, even today."

"What about the demons?" Mel said, her voice quavering.

He gave her a smile he hoped was reassuring, though with his face he could never be too sure.

"Sorry, I can talk too much."

From over by the bar, MAR-A said, "He does."

That made Mel giggle, so Jules appreciated it. "There are spirits in the other dimension that don't seem to have come from living things. As far as we can surmize, they evolved in that other realm. If something has never lived in our universe, we call it an in-human spirit, or demon."

"Why?" Sara asked.

"Our religions describe the demonic. There have been people that try to connect with demonic forces. As we discovered the reality of the spiritual ecosystem, we also learned that there was truth to those stories. It was during the Butlerian reconciliation of religion and science that we started to understand the connections between our dimensions."

Tee said, "Fine. Assume that's the worst case. What can you do about it?"

"I won't know until I learn what we're dealing with," Jules said. "If there is a demonic force, we might be able to do a cleansing to weaken the connection it has with you. Or it might be able to capture the entity or entities and contain them."

He reached up and ran a finger down the bone beads in his hair. "Sometimes it takes finding a resolution to weaken the spirit's hold on this dimension so they can move on."

"What if none of that works?" Sara said, her voice tight.

He looked at her for a second. She was brave. She wanted to protect her family. He felt her fierce desire to keep them safe.

"If MAR-A and I can't handle it," he said. "Then we'll ask someone else for help."

He prayed it wouldn't come to that. He didn't want to fail this family.

Chapter 13

THE MOOD IN THE common area had dropped. And along with that, the presence he sensed appeared to grow brighter. The tendrils remained dark to his other sight, yet appeared to glow with a dead light. It disturbed him, but he didn't think it was the main problem. Energy and emotions could draw presences, but this didn't seem like something that could arrange the trap in the airlock. That was something else.

Jules pushed to his feet. He took another drink from the frosty cold glass and then put it down on the dark composite table.

"Ready?" he said to Tee.

She nodded, pushing up off the arm of the couch. "Yeah. Let's do it."

She walked around the back of the couch and bent, quickly kissing the tops of the girls heads. Bri lifted her face and Tee kissed her on the lips, slow and lingering. Mel started giggling again.

The kiss broke apart. Tee said, "I'm so happy you're home. Love you."

"Love you too," Bri said.

Tee straightened and beckoned to Jules. "Come on, Jules. Let me give you the tour of our haunted house."

He followed her around the couch. She walked over to where MAR-A sat on the bar stool and surprised Jules by clapping a hand on MAR-A's shoulder.

"Want to come?"

MAR-A's head swung back and forth. "I can see through the system."

Tee shrugged. "Okay." Then, over her shoulder to Jules, "we'll start in the basement and work our way up."

She walked around the front of the bar to a hatch in the wall. Jules walked with her. As she entered a code to open the hatch, he said, "Basement?"

"It's the storage area beneath the commmon room." The hatch slid open, showing a landing and a ramp that curved down.

He followed her through. Once inside, she turned and secured the hatch.

"I keep it locked," Tee said. "I don't want the girls to end up down here. If I don't keep it locked, it opens on its own."

They started down the ramp. The air was colder here. His breath fogged the air in front of him. Tee noticed.

"That's part of it—I haven't been able to keep this section of the pod warm. I think I've fixed it and then the temperature drops."

"MAR-A might be able to help track the issue," Jules said.

Tee shrugged. "Great, if it can. The system goes offline for no reason that I can find. And sometimes there's a smell, like rotting meat."

"Meat?" Jules said, surprised.

"Yep. Even though we don't have any meat aboard. I don't know anyone that would. Everything we eat is plant-based."

"I guess meat-eating is still practiced on some planets," Jules said.

"By humans?"

He nodded. "Some groups still do."

"That's so gross. Well, not here. The first time I smelled it, I was sure that I was going to find a body from the previous crew. Maybe someone hid down here, froze, and was thawing out now that I had the systems up. I couldn't find anything and the smell went away. But it has come back several times since."

Though cold, the air smelled clean and fresh now. The light panels were dimmer than upstairs, but light enough to see clearly. They reached the bottom and another locked hatch.

Tee opened it and stepped through. Jules followed.

The space looked like it spanned the inner width of the pod. An aisle continued straight across, intersected twice with other aisles. In between were metal storage cages. With a regular crew, the cages would probably be assigned to different people to store belongings that wouldn't fit in the cabins above. Most of the cages contained an assortment of crates, shelves, and other items. One nearby held a hardshell spacesuit in a rack, the dull orange surface scratched and worn with use. Though supported in pieces on the rack, it still was disturbing.

Tee noticed his gaze. "That's for surface work. If you had to go out on a comet surface. The hard shell protects against debris impact that might puncture a standard suit."

He gestured at the room. "Have you gone through all of this?"

Tee shook her head. "No. Barely poked around. It hasn't been a priority."

Jules walked out into the aisle and moved along it. Tee followed.

"Anything other than the cold and smell happen down here?"

"Yeah."

He stopped, turning to look at her. She crossed her arms, rubbing them. He waited for her to gather herself.

"Sounds, mostly," Tee said. "Like someone was down here. The clank of a cage gate. Rustling. Once it sounded like people whispering back there." She pointed off across the room. She crossed her arms again.

"You'll think I'm crazy," Tee said. Her blue eyes looked at me and flicked away. Not, Jules thought, because of the uncanny look of his face.

"I doubt that," he said. He lifted a hand, indicating his face. "I've encountered things you wouldn't believe."

Her eyes flicked across his face, studying it. "I haven't seen a prosthetic like yours."

"It's Atorian-made," Jules said. "Artificial cellular structure driven by my facial muscles. It doesn't *quite* pull it off. People can tell it isn't real. It bothers them."

"It's a good face," she said.

"Thank you."

She took a breath. "I haven't told Bri about this. It happened right after she left to get help. I didn't want to worry her."

Tee shivered and looked around at the basement. "Do you need to see more? I'd rather not talk about it here."

"That's fine," Jules said. "Tell me about it later. Why don't you wait here and I'll take a look around?"

"By yourself?" She sounded more alarmed by that idea.

He nodded. "My presence might stir things up."

"Why?"

"Because we're a threat to them, MAR-A and I. Our presence often gets a reaction. But that's good, because it can tell us what we're dealing with."

"Okay," she said. Her tone indicated doubt.

Jules couldn't think of anything else to tell her that would make her feel better, so he didn't try.

He started down the aisle and reached out with his sense. The basement seemed quiet right now. The disturbances Tee had described could be an active imagination, outright fabrications, or they could indicate the presence of spirits. He had to consider all of the options. He didn't see any reason the family would try to fabricate the stories about the ship. It wasn't likely to help them in any way he could see.

The basement would have been creepy without any ghost stories. The center cages were square, while the outer ones curved to match the curve of the pod. It was all one big room. Down the aisle on his left, he discovered the lifts. They must be the same lift shafts that went up to the common area and the cabins. They sat at the junction of the aisles, the corners clipped on the cages with flat segments to make room for the lifts.

Off to his right, he heard a footstep drag on the floor.

Jules stopped and turned in that direction. He didn't see anything, but the sensation of being *watched* raised hairs on the back of his neck.

The sound came again. A long, dragging sound of a foot against the floor panels. He went in that direction and reached out with his other senses, probing for what might be around the corner.

It seemed like nothing was there, but he had heard those steps. Had been *meant* to hear them, he thought.

He walked quickly around the corner and nearly coiled with the tall hooded shape. MAR-A's skull-like head shoved forward.

"I scared you."

Jules shook his head, looking up at the droid. "Why are you down here?"

"Say I scared you."

"I scared you," Jules said.

MAR-A made a hissing noise like a scalded cat and hunched its shoulders.

"You came down for a reason, or just to try and scare me?"

"A reason," MAR-A said, his words crackling with electric discharges. "The cameras for the basement are out. I couldn't see anything. I needed to ascertain what was happening here."

"And have you learned anything?"

After a moment's hesitation, "No. There wasn't–"

"Time? You'd better not say that."

"An opportunity," MAR-A drew in their arms. "I haven't examined the equipment yet."

"Because you're trying to scare me."

"I will begin my inspection."

"Great. Do that instead of messing around."

Jules wasn't getting anything else from the basement. He headed back toward Tee and found her in the open hatch to the ramp, looking like she was ready to bolt.

He waved to her, and she stepped back into the basement. "What was that? You talked to it?"

He nodded. "MAR-A came down to inspect cameras. It wasn't getting the feed."

The tension in her shoulders eased. "They keep dropping out all over the ship. I get one fixed and another *three* go down. If they can figure it out, that'd be great."

"MAR-A is good at that sort of thing," Jules said. He gestured at the hatch.

Tee hesitated a second, then said. "Actually, let's take the lift down to the sub-basement. We can talk there."

"Sub-basement?"

"It's where the environmental systems are located. The main units for water and air recycling, temperature and humidity regulation." She closed the hatch to the ramp. "Let's be quick."

She started up the aisle at a quick pace Jules matched. Her head didn't stop moving, checking all around them as they went up the aisle and turned to go to the lifts.

"MAR-A is around here somewhere," Jules said. "Hopefully they won't jump out at us."

Tee laughed nervously. "Yeah, that wouldn't be great."

Whatever had scared her, they reached the lifts without incident. While they waited for the lift to reach them, Jules caught a glimpse of MAR-A moving behind one of the cages before the droid's path took it behind crates staked there.

A chime announced the lift arrival and the doors opened. Tee hurried in. Jules followed. She touched the sub-basement icon and stepped back, leaning against the back wall, as the doors closed. He heard her sigh when the lift started moving.

It didn't travel far before it stopped with another chime as it reached the sub-basement.

Tee pushed off the back wall and strode out, looking much more relaxed now.

The space outside the lift was a narrow corridor with bundles of pipes and wires suspended along the ceiling above. A short distance ahead it reached an intersection with a perpendicular corridor that must serve as a sort of control center. It was round, with four consoles in the arcs between the corridors. Circular light panels glowed in the ceiling above, hanging beneath the pipes and wires that ran along the corridors.

Tee pulled one of the chairs away from the console–it rode on a sort of armature that gave it some range of movement and placement, and sat down, spinning to face him.

Jules took the chair from the opposite console. As he sat, the height adjusted so his feet rested lightly on the floor. He folded his hands and waited for her to tell him her story.

Chapter 14

THREE DAYS AFTER BRI left, I went down to the basement to put away some sealant I'd gotten from one of the other pods I was bringing online. The former crew had plenty of supplies, mostly stored in dedicated storage pods. I wanted to move some of it to each of the pods I brought online. That way, if there was a problem in a pod, I'd have the supplies I needed in the same pod. With a larger crew it's different. With me doing most of the work, I can't count on having time to run off to a storage pod to get what I needed. I wanted to plan for the worst case scenario, if the pod I was in was cut off from the others.

Emergency sealant was one item I definitely wanted available in each pod. I have repair bots, but they need supervision and I haven't checked them out yet. Many of them were offline when we boarded.

I had four canisters of emergency sealant on an autotrolley. Each one is over 100 kilos. I took the lift so I didn't have to mess around with hatches.

It was late. I was tired. I got down to the basement with the trolley and went to the first cage on the right. I wanted the cans right in front by the door so I could get to them quickly if I needed them.

The cage door didn't want to open. It asked for a code. I gave it the code. And it denied it.

That shouldn't be possible because I'd reset all of the codes on the ship and my code has the highest level of clearance.

I'd made a mistake, I thought. I tried again. It didn't work.

I started to put it in again when I heard the crying.

At first, I thought it was one of the girls–there's no one else here–but it sounded *weird*. Almost like a baby crying, gasping for air between cries. I wasn't thinking about that then, only that one of the girls must have hurt themselves and needed help.

I left the trolley and sealant. I went down the aisle toward the intersection.

"Sarah? Mel? Where are you?" I called out.

The crying continued as if they hadn't heard me. Which might not be surprising because it was sounding more and more terrified. A high-pitched wailing, almost screams.

I called louder. "Sarah! Mel!"

The crying turned into shrieks. I was crying now, sobbing, as I ran down the aisles, looking down the cross aisles, and not finding anything. I called out to them again and again, but it seemed like instead of hearing me they were becoming more and more frantic. It was screams, no doubt now, and it sounded like they were being tortured, like they were in agony.

After turning corners and running up and down aisles, I still couldn't place where the cries were coming from. It always sounded like it was ahead of me, no matter what way I went.

"Where are you?" I called. "I can't find you!"

I wasn't thinking anymore, or I would have realized that this couldn't be happening.

I grabbed the cage wire at a corner, using it to sling myself around the corner back into the next aisle where it sounded like the cries were coming from. As I swung around, I saw something in the cage I'd grabbed.

It was a person under a sheet, lying in their back across crates in the cage. The front of the sheet was wet and red with blood in a massive splatter across the front. As soon as I saw it, the screams and cries ceased instantly.

It took a couple seconds before a registered that it had stopped because it had penetrated so deep into my awareness.

I was frozen, clutching at the cage wire, staring at the silent body beneath the sheet. Based on the size, it had to be Sarah. Mel was too small. But it didn't look right for Sarah either, only I got the odd idea it was because of what had happened to her. The body just lay there, so still, covered with that bloody sheet. The blood made it look as if her chest had been ripped open. It had to be Sarah, there wasn't anyone else on board that it could be. We'd have noticed if there were survivors on the ship.

I finally got up the courage to go to the cage door. I touched the command to open the cage and it clicked, unlocking. The door slid out of my way.

With the way open, I didn't want to see. I was sobbing, begging that it wasn't Sarah. I was sure it couldn't be Mel because of the size, but it was hard to shake the feeling that it was Sarah.

Before I stepped into the cage, my foot was raised, about to take that step, there was a sigh of air from the body. It rippled around the body's head.

I didn't take the step.

I put my foot back down as the strangeness of the situation sank in and my panic ebbed. How could this be Sarah? It didn't make sense. This was some sort of trick. It had to be.

I didn't take the step. Instead, I grabbed the door and pulled it closed. The clang echoed through the basement.

On the crates in the cage, the body sat up and turned its head in my direction. The sheet started to slip.

I backed away from the cage, then glanced nervously behind me. That cage had the usual assortment of crates and clutter. No medical units that could help the person beneath the sheet. Even though they were probably beyond help.

The sheet continued to slither off the person's head, pooling in their lap. The last bit of it slipped up past their shoulders–I saw a hint of long dark hair beneath it, and then the last part slid over the top of their head and fell.

There was nothing beneath. The sheet crumpled onto the top of the crates as if it had been tossed there. There was still blood visible on the sheet, but obviously nothing beneath it.

I ran.

At first I couldn't figure out where the lifts were, I'd gotten so turned around. I skidded around a corner and saw the lifts. And the canisters that had been the reason for coming down here had been knocked off the auto trolley. None had ruptured, but they lay in the path to the lifts.

I didn't slow down. I didn't stop. I dodged between the fallen canisters, afraid they would move and trip me, but they didn't. I got to the lift and pressed the call button.

It should have been on this level, unless someone had used it, but according to the indicator on the panel it was coming down from the attic.

I resisted the urge to pound uselessly on the button and instead slapped the wall. "Come on, come on."

A loud sizzling noise sounded behind me. I spun around, seeing only the empty aisles leading out from the lift. Only the lights were out now around the perimeter.

I looked at the indicator. The lift was coming, but it seemed impossibly slow. At the far end of the aisle directly in front of the lift, just inside the shadows since the lights were out, there was a person standing there beneath a sheet. Exactly like what I saw in the cage, including the blood soaking the sheet.

I looked at the other aisles and saw another sheeted figure in both. Not identical to the first. One was taller, as tall as the combat droid, but still covered beneath the sheet. The other was as wide as two people. The sheet didn't cover it entirely, revealing fat gray arms beneath the edge of the sheet. But all of the sheets were bloody.

Another electric sizzling noise and the next ring of lights flickered and died. The shadows advanced and the figures were just *there* at the edge of the shadows.

The lift arrived and I stumbled back into it. I didn't look away from the figures. I hit the panel by feel, selecting the common area. I had to find our girls, make sure they were safe from whatever this was.

The sheeted apparitions started weeping as the lift doors closed.

I *felt* the lift move up to the common area. I leaned against the doors, catching my breath, trying to understand what had just happened.

The lift chimed as it reached the common area. I dropped my arms and when the doors open I hurried out to find the girls.

I walked right into a sealant canister and tripped over it. I sprawled forward and hit hard enough to nearly knock out my breath.

Groaning, I pushed myself up and immediately saw that I was in the basement, not the common area.

The electric snapping, sizzling sounded over the weeping from the figures. The next ring of lights went out–leaving only two left around the lifts. I scrambled back, crawling back but got fouled on the canister that I'd tripped over.

A loud crackling and popping came from the lights and the next ring went out. The whole basement was dark except for the small remaining circle of light.

They still stood at the edge of the light shrouded in their sheets. The blood on the sheets was running down the folds, soaking closer to the floor. They sobbed and cried wordlessly.

I kicked and got away from the canister. I scrambled to my feet and backed into the lift. I touched the panel for the common room again.

The doors closed but I could still see out through the hexagon windows in the doors.

The lift started up. I watched this time. I saw the basement dropping away, the single ring of light below, the figure in the center aisle still unmoving at the edge of the light.

The lift rose up into darkness. It came to a stop as the light vanished. All that remained was the light from the ceiling panels. The common area was pitch black, the light reflected from the windows so I couldn't see out.

The doors opened and the light from the lift lit the spilled canisters on the floor.

I was back in the basement. The last ring of light was out and the sheeted figures stood close, at the edge of the light from the lift.

It wouldn't last.

I darted from the lift. I jumped over the canisters and dove between two of the apparitions. It wasn't graceful. I rolled clumsily, scrambled to my feet, and darted into the dark aisles.

The cages rattled around me as if something was trying to get out. I skidded around the corner at the intersection, going on memory and feel only.

I was sure I was going to run into something in that darkness. I did. It was the hatch. The one to the ramp that we came down. The panel was dark. No power remained.

The cage rattling stopped. I heard the rustle of sheets on the floor and I *knew* the apparitions were coming.

The manual release panel was where I pictured it. I dug my fingers into the edges and pulled it free. Inside I found the release and twisted it in the release combination. The hatch release clicked. I spun the wheel enough to open the hatch. Light blinded me. I opened it far enough to squeeze through.

I *felt* their presences behind me. I expected any seconds to feel their hands on me, pulling me back into the basement. I squirmed through the opening, jerked my way through to the other side, falling as I did into the lit corridor. I kicked and scrambled back, pressing myself against the wall.

I stared at the slice of darkness past the hatch. Out of that dark, came the sound of a child crying.

That was it. I pushed up the wall and ran up the ramp to the common area. I couldn't open the hatch fast enough.

When it opened, I flinched back, expecting darkness but everything was bright and normal. Sarah was walking across the room with a glass of juice. Mel was on the couch studying.

Sarah looked at me, frowned, and said, "Mama Tee? Are you okay? Did you see a ghost?"

Mel dropped her tablet and turned around on the couch, eyes bright. "Did you?"

I laughed, shook my head, and did my best to look unconcerned. I probably wasn't convincing. I lied to my girls.

"But stay out of the basement," I told them after reassuring them again that I *hadn't* seen a ghost. "We're having some power relay issues and trouble with the lights. I wouldn't want you stuck down there."

After that, I kept the hatch secured and removed their access to the basement on the lift.

I didn't want to scare them, or Bri, so I didn't say anything.

Chapter 15

THE SUB-BASEMENT HUMMED WITH the sounds of the equipment functioning to keep the pod alive. Screens showed readouts of various measures. Tee looked at her hands after she finished her story.

It was...*disturbing*. Frightening. Between her story and the one Bri had shared, along with the video, about the figure in the airlock, it suggested something worse than he'd seen before.

"Did cameras in the basement capture any of this?"

Tee looked up, eyes flashing. "No. But it happened like I told you."

He spread his hands, palms out. "I'm not disputing it. Bri showed me the airlock video. I wondered if you had something like it."

Tee quirked her lips. "Sorry. It just all sounds crazy. If one of the girls had told me the same thing, I don't know if I'd believe it. Before, I mean."

"Makes sense. Things like this are rare."

"Be careful what you wish for," Tee said sourly. "If it sounds too good to be true and all of that shit. That's what this feels like. We thought we had this wonderful opportunity to do what we'd always dreamed. Should have known better."

He shook his head. "You couldn't expect this."

"Couldn't we?" She studied him for a couple seconds. "We could have asked for a spiritual inspection, couldn't we?"

"If it had occurred to you. But that's not standard."

"If those assholes on Alyx Salvage had done a proper inspection, it might have saved us some trouble."

Jules wasn't going to argue the point. He wanted to get back to her story. "After this happened, when did you go back to the basement?"

Tee rocked forward and clasped her hands. "The next day. I took the ramp. Everything was normal. Lights, temperature, there wasn't anything unusual."

"And the canisters of sealant?"

"Still dumped on the floor. But no signs of blood or the sheets. I put the canisters into the cage and got the hell out of there."

"And you've been back since then? Anything else happen?"

Tee shook her head. "I've stayed out as much as possible. The other times, same thing. I took the ramp, didn't trust the lift, and got out right away. I *thought* I heard something one time, like someone breathing in another aisle and I got out of there quick. But that one could have been my imagination."

Jules gestured at the sub-basement around them. "But no problems down here?"

Tee shook her head. "No. Is there a reason for that?"

Jules shrugged. "I don't know."

"What must have happened to the previous crew to cause all of this?"

"It may not originate with them," Jules said. "We don't know what happened here. Not yet. I'll figure out what's going on and how to put a stop to it."

Tee laughed. "If you can, that'd be wonderful. I kept thinking we should have all gone with Bri after what happened in the basement. Become stationers. But now that she's back, I don't want to do that. Not if there's another way."

"That's what need to find," Jules said. He stood. "Ready to show me the rest of the ship?"

Tee stood up. "Yeah. Let's do it."

They took the lift back up to the common area. Bri and the girls were still on the couch, laughing and talking, which stopped as they stepped out of the lift. MAR-A was back on the bar stool again, looking as if they had never moved from the spot.

Still smiling, Bri said, "Everything okay?"

"Yes," Tee said. "Just giving Jules the full tour."

There was more to see on this level. In addition to the central common area, there was more around it. The passage that circled the common area mirrored the one on the floor above, where the cabins were located. The spaces on this floor included the kitchens, dining area, exercise facilities, a small medical area took up several sections, and then there were additional offices. It was becoming apparent that the ship was much, much larger than it had seemed. And meant for a much larger crew.

"How can you run a ship this big without more crew?"

Tee shrugged. "No choice right now. I have the bots to help. But mostly, we're only running at a few percent capacity."

They reached another intersection in the corridor. It looked like the passage that went out to the airlock, but Jules didn't think that they'd gone around that far yet. "Does that lead to the next pod?"

Tee nodded. "The pods are linked together around the ship. There are four habitation pods like this one, out of thirty-six. They're spaced around the ship, each taking a shift in turn so that the ship can operate continuously while giving the crew days off."

"Have you been to the other habitation pods?"

Tee shook her head. "No."

Jules stopped and turned, looking at her. He couldn't tell if his surprise showed on his face, or not. "Could there be people out there, in other pods?"

"No," she said, shaking her head. "Most of the pods are unpowered, except for the ones I've brought online. If there was anyone there–they're not alive now. This ship is large, it's a comet miner. But my priority has been getting what we need secure and running."

"There might be answers to what happened in some of those pods."

Tee started walking. He matched her stride, seeing that she needed to move, to release the energy she felt. They came to the ramp leading to the next level, and she started up.

"I know. I've wanted to investigate more. All I've had time to do is send a bot around the ring. It went from pod to pod, straight through, it didn't explore. It's main purpose was to check the integrity. Did the pods have power? Atmosphere? Everything was at standby, minimal systems. Five pods didn't have pressure, including one of the habitation pods. The rest appeared more or less intact."

They reached the next level where the cabins were.

"Can you show me the girl's first room? The one that had the strange odor?"

"Sure. That was weird. I couldn't figure out a source for the odor."

It wasn't far. Tee stopped outside the cabin door. She entered a code on the panel and the door opened.

It looked much like the cabin they'd given him. He stepped inside and inhaled. It didn't have any noticeable odor.

Tee had followed him inside. "It doesn't stay. It comes and goes."

With his other sense, Jules reached out into the room. There was something. He couldn't see it, like something seen out of the corner of his eye, but gone when he turned his head. The room had two bunks, blankets rumpled and left that way. No other signs of habitation. The sense of something there, just out of view persisted.

Tee was watching him. "Anything?"

"I'm not sure," he said. He started back to the door. "What's next?"

"Attic," Tee said.

It had its own lift, a short way down the corridor, with an unmarked door that looked more like a closet than a lift. When Tee opened the door the space inside was small, round, and utilitarian. He followed her in and even standing on opposite sides of the lift, they were still standing close facing each other that they might have been dancing.

"Sorry, it's meant mostly for the bots."

"That's okay." He looked up as the lift moved, even though there was nothing to see. "What's up here?"

"The pod's brains," Tee said. "It has multiple servers handling the network, systems, coordinating the bots, and the connection to the rest of the ship."

The lift was slowing as Jules said, "It sounds like the pods could function independently."

"That's the idea," Tee said. "Modular, mostly self-contained, interchangeable. The interior structures can be disassembled and reused in different configurations. The pods have limited propulsion. Maneuvaring thrusters used primarily when rearranging the order of pods in the ship's ring."

The lift stopped completely and the door opened on a small hallway, dimly lit. It was only a little wider than the lift. Compared to the rest of the pod, even the sub-basement, it was a cramped space. Jules walked out with Tee following. The aisle ended a short distance ahead as the passage opened up into a larger space. He stepped out, studying the shadowed distances.

They were under a dome with a few hexagonal light panels glowing with a dim blue light. It looked like a warehouse. Crates were stacked in towers of varying heights in the space around the dome. There were other structures in the distance with a myriad of small lights, but he couldn't make out the details. He shifted his vision spectrum and the "attic" came into better view.

The equipment around the walls must house the servers and other associated equipment. The equipment stood in sections with space between them.

The low-light vision stripped away the saturation in the scene, making it duller, but brighter. The crates, weren't crates at all. It was the bots. Stacks of them. Legs and limbs folded up, bodies blocky. Sensors and ports decorating their sides. The seemed inactive. Similar to some of the bots he'd seen before on the station, but a bit flatter. He thought of crabs stacked one on the top of the next.

Tee stood beside him, rubbing her arms. "I don't come up here often."

He *looked*, using his other sense of the place. A shadow moved behind one of the stacks. His breath fogged the air. It was colder up here.

"Is it always cold up here?"

"No," Tee said, sounding annoyed. "Normally we have to cool it, given the heat generated by the equipment and bots. It shouldn't be this cold."

Another shadow shifted behind the stacks of droids. He looked at all of the blank lenses on the dormant bots.

Hairs on his neck and arms crawled with the sensation of being watched.

"What do you see?" Tee said, rubbing her arms.

The shadowy beings, whatever they were, slipped from place to place in silence. He caught a glimpse of a dark long-fingered hand on a bot and then it was gone. Shadowy, blackened, and odd somehow, but hard to see in the dim blue light.

He motioned Tee back. "We should go."

"What is it? What's there?"

A smell like rotting meat, decaying vegetation, and sewage forced its way into his nose and mouth, making him gag with sudden revulsion.

Tee made retching sounds and moved back into the passed. "What is that?"

"Go," he said, fighting not to breath through his nose. "Back to the lift."

She didn't protest. She coughed and made a gagging noise as she turned and started back to the lift.

Jules stepped back into the passage.

On one of the closest piles of bots, the one on top suddenly tumbled sidewise off the top of the stack. It activated in mid-air, uncurled its feet and landed as nimbly as a cat. UV lights shone out from its square body directly at Jules. The light momentarily blinded his vision.

He lifted his arm to block it and heard the sound of more bots hitting the floor.

Chapter 16

THE NARROWNESS OF THE passage would make it difficult for too many of the bots to reach them at once. But Jules wasn't planning on sticking around to see what the bots were going to do.

"They shouldn't be doing that," Tee said behind him.

"Maybe, but they are," he said. "Get into the lift."

"They won't harm us. They have safety protocols to enforce it."

Out on the attic floor the bots crawled smoothly forward on their legs. It wasn't the most graceful motion. They jerked back and forth as each leg snapped out. Their UV lights kept sweeping across the passage as they crawled quickly forward.

This wasn't looking good. "I don't know if those protocols are working."

Tee was retreating back down the passage. He kept backing up, facing the opening and the oncoming bots. Whatever else had been out there, he couldn't see it now.

His shoulder bumped into the side of the lift opening. He turned sideways and slipped in facing Tee. She touched the panel and the lift dropped downward. She gave him a frightened look.

"They shouldn't have activated on their own. They aren't sentient, only bots. Tools."

Jules sent a text to MAR-A. *Was that you?*

The reply was instant. *No. There was a disruption in the bot instruction sets. I'm shutting them down.*

"MAR-A is turning them off," he told Tee. "Something disrupted their instruction sets."

"What you saw up there?"

"Maybe," he said. "Spirits sometimes move objects, or use them as a conduit."

"And the bots count as objects?"

"As much as a doll or a hatch," he said. "I've seen similar things happen before."

He didn't add that those situations had been among the worst that he had dealt with. Whatever was happening on the *Olympia*, it wasn't going to be easy to resolve. He didn't like the glimpses he'd gotten in the attic.

The lift reached the floor below. Tee went first and immediately headed back towards the ramp down to the common area. He followed and quickly checked with MAR-A.

*Progress?"

The disruption has ceased. Bots are back in standby mode.

"MAR-A has the bots back in standby," he told Tee as they started down.

"Good. I'm going to review the logs. I need to figure out what happened. And how to stop it from happening again."

Did that scare you? MAR-A texted.

No, Jules sent.

"Because it looked like it scared you," MAR-A sent.

He ignored that and sent, *What caused it?*

Unable to identify at this time.

Of course not. Jules breathed in and let it out again. They reached the bottom of the ramp and took the short passage to the common area. Bri twisted around as they entered, grinning as she said, "How's the tour going?"

Tee shook her head. She headed to the bar and grabbed a tablet lying there. "Something tried to send the bots after us."

That brought Bri up off the couch, coming around the furniture. The girls exclaimed and twisted around on the couch, looking at Jules and their parents.

"I stopped them," MAR-A announced from its seat at the bar.

"That's good," Bri said, before turning back to Tee. "You're okay?"

"Yes," Tee said, squeezing her hand. "We got out of there before anything happened."

Jules took a seat on another stool where he could see everyone. In his other sight, the streamers of darkness still coiled around the family. Slow, sinuous motions that made his gut queasy.

Sara swung up onto the back of the couch, sitting there braced with both hands. Mel immediately scrambled up and copied her. Bri and Tee stood together on one side, their attention on him.

"What are we dealing with, Jules?" Bri said.

"I believe there are many spirits here," he said. "Most of them probably wouldn't draw any notice. But since I arrived and opened myself to the spiritual ecosystem on board, I've seen other things. Inhuman spirits that are gathered around your family."

"Why?" Mel said. Sara tried to shush her.

Jules lifted a hand, palm up. "You've entered their home. The *Olympia* is like an oasis in space. Ships and stations do that, not only for living things like us, but for non-living beings as well. Usually that isn't a problem."

"But it is this time," Tee said, not asking.

"Right," Jules said. The girls and their parents were scared. He didn't want to scare them, but they also needed to know what might happen. "These inhuman spirits are drawn to your energy. After all this time, there are complex living things they can draw energy from. They want it all, including your souls."

Bri hugged Tee close. Then as one, they moved over to the couch. They divided and each took a seat beside the girls on the back of the couch, hugging their daughters.

"That's not nice," Mel declared.

MAR-A shifted, turning on the bar stool. "They don't concern themselves with *nice*."

"They should," Mel said.

"They don't," MAR-A said.

Mel crossed her arms and said, "But they should."

Jules held out his hands toward the combat droid and the small girl. "You're both right. Since they should be nice and aren't, we're going to have to stop them."

"You can do that?" Sara said.

If things went as he hoped. "Yes," he said. "I believe that we can. Together. It's going to take all of you too. This is your home, so you'll need to help with the solution."

"Of course," Tee said, squeezing Mel closer. "What do you need us to do?"

"Support each other. Look out for each other," Jules said. "If you experience anything strange, tell me, MAR-A, or one of your mothers. Meanwhile, MAR-A is taking care of watching the systems. I'll do so as well, and start laying the groundwork that will either banish these spirits, or render them harmless."

Sara appeared convinced. She nodded.

"Good," Jules said. Belief was important. It had always been that way. Religious rituals allowed people to focus their energy to interact with the spiritual world. As a Butlerian, Jules knew how crucial faith could be in human endeavors. Without it, humanity wouldn't have made it over the great hurdle, and out to the stars. Except for the fael, who apparently lacked any innate connection to the spiritual world, the species that spread to the stars understood the intersection of material and non-material. Without that full picture of the universe, it was hard to see how a species could make that leap. Humanity had wondered where everyone was in centuries past without understanding the scope of the problem.

The Makkars gathered together, talking softly. He left them to it and turned back to MAR-A.

"Everything calm in the attic now?"

"Yes," MAR-A said. "I completed and inventory check of all bots in this pod. It apears to include most of the bot inventory on the ship."

"All here?" Jules glanced over at Tee. "I guess that makes sense with her working alone."

MAR-A hissed. Jules looked at the droid. Every noise it made was deliberate.

"What is it?"

"I don't understand these humans," MAR-A said.

"What about them?"

"They come here alone. Without sufficient crew. It is unsafe."

"It's a risk," Jules said. "One they chose to take to be free."

MAR-A said, "They weren't free before?"

"Yes, to an extent. Within limits. You know what that's like."

"It's different for humans."

"Yes and no," Jules said. "It isn't easy to break out of debt, launch your own enterprise, secure your own future. I admire them for trying."

MAR-A turned its head, lenses looking–Jules thought–at Mel. "But did the children make that choice?"

"They're with their parents. That's what counts. They aren't developed enough to make their own choices."

MAR-A looked at Jules. The metal head beneath the hood superficially resembled a human skull, though the proportions were wrong and the face too flat. Still chilling. The lights around the lenses rotated.

Jules looked back, wondering at the thoughts within the droid's crystalline pathways. It was a person under the law. Recognized as fundamentally different than the utility bots up in the attic. Not exactly alive, but intelligent. A bit like an inhuman spirit. Something that had never been alive, but imbued with purpose. The combat droids original purpose was a war they didn't start and one that they eventually refused to fight, even though it meant the destruction of most.

Looking at MAR-A, Jules knew that *someone* was looking back, but it was an order of intelligence that he couldn't understand. And as far as anyone could tell, lacked a connection to the spiritual plane of the universe.

Given all of that, he trusted MAR-A. The droid chose to help him, to help others. That, at least, was a comfort. He couldn't know if MAR-A felt concern for the girls in the same way, but there was something there.

"How much of the ship do you have access to now?" Jules said.

"Sixteen percent."

"What's the status of the rest?"

"Offline."

"Let's keep it that way," Jules said. "We'll keep our investigation in the active sections for now."

"Agreed."

Bri came over to them. "We're going to begin making dinner, if that's okay?"

"Sounds wonderful," Jules said. His stomach growled in agreement.

Bri looked at MAR-A. "Is there anything we can do for you? Anything you'd like?"

"Permission to use the repair bots to upgrade or enhance my monitoring?"

"I don't see why not, but let's ask Tee." Bri beckoned to Tee.

The engineer joined them, slipping an arm around Bri's waist. "Yes?"

Bri repeated MAR-A's request. Tee nodded and looked up at the combat droid. "Yes, thanks. That'd be great."

"Thank you," MAR-A said. The lights dimmed around its lenses as it sat back.

Tee turned to Jules. "Pasta okay?"

He nodded. "Sounds wonderful."

"Great," Bri said. "Why don't you make yourself comfortable, rest, and we'll take care of dinner."

Tee shook her head. "The girls and I will handle dinner. *You* also spent the day traveling and should rest too."

Bri kissed her lightly. "Fine. I'll look at my reports."

"That's work, not rest."

"It's restful for me," Bri said.

Jules stood. "I think I'll go back to my cabin until dinner."

He waved to the girls and crossed the room to the ramp entrance before starting up. He thought he might avoid the lift, unless it was necessary.

Chapter 17

J ULES SETTLED ON THE edge of the bunk in his cabin and took several deep breaths to center himself. Weariness tugged at him like fingers trying to pull him back into the bunk. It'd been a long time since he'd had anyone trying to coax him back to bed. As challenging as it was living in the uncanny valley, he knew that wasn't the real reason. There'd be plenty of people that would adjust to how he looked.

He breathed in through his nose and out through his mouth.

He let the thoughts of companionship slip away. It'd been a long trip to get here. He was tired, but more than that, disturbed by the intensity of events happening on this ship.

He breathed and let his eyes closed. He pictured the ship the way he had seen it on approach. The pods looking deceptively small between the inner and outer rings of the spinning ship. Robotic arms extended from the inner rings to the captured comet at the center. It didn't rotate. The arms compensated for the rotation of the ship to keep their position in relation to the comet. Several arms worked on the comet, but the larger pits caused by the main arms looked like eye sockets in the icy shape. The distorted end of the comet suggested a broken jaw area with teeth.

The sunlight fell across the ship, illuminating most of the rings and pods, except where the shadows fell. The leading rings extended back away from the comet in a conical tail leading to the drive section. Solar sails extended out from the drive in enormous wings that dwarfed the big comet harvester.

[cycle back and update the description of the ship] He breathed in and out. In his mind, the ship rotated. It was the rotation that pressed him into the bunk.

Always in movement.

There was more to what was going on with the *Olympia* than the entity or entities that he had sensed. What had happened to the previous crew? It wouldn't be the first time that a ship had turned up empty. The *Ridley, Kiason,* and the *Awotwi* that he knew about. Surely there had been others. Causes varied. Ships had even turned up with crew missing clear back when they were sailing vessels on Earth.

Jules breathed in and out, letting the thoughts flow. He was open, receptive. Not trying to force a connection with the other plane, but accepting it if something wanted to communicate. It was a risk to do this alone, but he wanted to keep the family out of it if he could.

He sensed presences. Distant awareness like the sound of something rustling in the bushes.

Structures, whether in space or on a planet, could act like an artificial reef for the spiritual ecosystem. The energy of living things, of the ship itself, was like an underwater geothermal vent providing energy for the population of organisms. Ships and structures did the same thing.

Usually it was harmless and unnoticed by the living.

Things that happened in a place could leave a stain. Draw malignant spirits, predators that preyed on others, including inhuman spirits. *Demons.*

That glimpse in the attic, that's what it felt like.

He heard the cabin door softly sliding open. Cold air swirled around him. Jules opened his eyes.

The door was partly open. In his thermal overlays, the air around the door was 10 degrees colder than the ambient temperature in the room. Streamers of cold extended forward from that spot, chilling the air.

He relayed what he was seeing to MAR-A.

"Nothing showing in the corridor cameras," MAR-A sent. "Limited range."

Jules focused on the spot just inside the door with his other sight as well. A sense of shadows clung to the area, obscuring it from view.

"An entity, undetermined nature, has opened my cabin door," Jules said for the recording of the encounter.

"Thermal output shows an amporhous region approximately 10 degrees colder than the surrounding air. Streamers of cold reach out from the main region."

Then, to the spirit, he said, "Do you want to communicate with us? Are you responsible for the disturbances on this ship?"

He sensed its attention focus on him briefly before flickering away. The cold region moved along the wall inside the cabin without approaching any closer.

"Speak to me," Jules urged. "Tell me what it is you want."

It gave no indication that it heard or understood him. The colder area continued to move along the wall. When it reached the corner it shrank away, as if moving *through* the wall, and then was gone.

Jules was off the bed in a second. He ran out of the cabin, sending to MAR-A. "Unlock the next cabin for me."

As he reached the door, the panel beside it changed to show it was unlocked. He touched the open command and the door slid to the side.

This was an unoccupied cabin, bare and lacking any sign of recent habitation. The area of cold didn't show on his overlays. He stepped inside and looked around the room to be sure.

He didn't sense anything. His eyes didn't see any noticeable temperature variations. It had *looked* like the cold spot was passing through the wall, but it must have faded instead as it neared the wall.

"Still not reading anything unusual," MAR-A sent, boredom indicated.

"There was something," Jules said aloud.

"If so," MAR-A answered, "I can get no reading of it."

Jules nodded. He couldn't either. The presence—whatever it had been—might have only been briefly in contact with this plane. Enough to trip the door sensor. Then it moved on.

Chapter 18

T HE PRESENCE JULES HAD followed into the next cabin was gone. At least he couldn't detect it any longer. The cabin air was dry, clean, and lacked the intense cold he'd felt when his cabin door opened.

MAR-A's messages were tagged with the boredom signifier. "Nothing there now."

"No," Jules agreed. He cast a final look around the cabin and then stepped back out into the corridor.

A tall shape swathed in dark robes towered over him as the door slid closed. He looked up at MAR-A's glittering lenses.

"You wanted to see for yourself?"

"I scared you," MAR-A said.

Jules sighed and turned to return to his cabin. MAR-A's long legs easily kept pace. His cabin door was closed.

He glanced back at MAR-A and nodded at the door. "Did you close this?"

"No."

He touched the panel. The door slid open. He looked inside, feeling MAR-A leaning over him to see.

He stepped into the cabin. Nothing looked touched. He didn't feel any cold air, or see anything else unusual. MAR-A followed him on into the room.

"I don't detect anything," MAR-A said.

Jules shook his head. "I don't either."

He might have closed the door when he left the room, he couldn't remember. If it was part of the disturbance, it was a much more mild example than the stories he'd already heard from Bri and Tee.

He sat in one of the chairs, leaning back with his legs extended, and looked up at MAR-A standing beside the bed.

"Were you able to access any records in the ship systems? Logs that explain what happened to the former crew?"

"I have a file recovery program running," MAR-A said. "Nothing yet."

"How many of habitation pods are active?"

"Only this one is active."

"Can we bring the others online? What is their condition?"

"Unknown," MAR-A said. "It would be safest to send repair bots to the pods and inspect them as they are."

That was true, but Jules had a feeling it wouldn't work. Too many things could go wrong. And without being there, he wouldn't be able to sense if there were other presences.

"I can't investigate from here," Jules said. "I need to be *there* if I'm going to sense anything."

"Then I will accompany you," MAR-A said. "It's the only way to make sure you don't end up dead."

Jules didn't plan to argue the point. Since he'd started working with MAR-A, the big combat droid had saved his skin more than once. Most of it, anyway. MAR-A couldn't have prevented what happened to his face. Saving his life was enough.

"So how do we get over to the other pods? Do we go through the pods in-between?"

"The *Olympia* is equipped with two transfer modules, one on each side that ride the rails around the ship," MAR-A said. "It's faster. We use one to make the transit to the pods you want to visit."

"Okay," Jules said. "We'll talk to Tee about it over dinner. If she's okay with the plan, then we go first thing in the morning."

"It would save time if you didn't need sleep," MAR-A said.

Right at that moment, Jules stifled a yawn. "You bet. I don't expect that to change."

Closing his eyes for a second, the urge to topple over onto the bed and sleep was strong. He fought it off. There was still work to do tonight. It was easier to ignore the need to sleep when he was younger. He never needed a nap then, but he could use one now.

He opened his eyes and looked up at MAR-A. "What else have you learned about the ship? Anything in the system?"

"The salvager report was cursory. The ship shows no overt signs of damage. The power core is stable. Solar sails show microimpact wear consistent with age. Fabrication and printing systems have sufficient raw materials in stock to produce whatever parts are required."

MAR-A paused. Jules knew it was giving him time to formulate any questions. He gestured for it to continue.

"Refinery pods are functional, one currently active to process the materials from the comet."

Jules remembered the somewhat skull-like appearance of the comet being mined. It was only his imagination, feeding off the situation.

MAR-A said, "One storage pod is active to take the materials extracted from the comet."

"So that's what, five pods in operation?"

"Six," MAR-A said. "This habitation pod, a refinery pod, storage pod, manufacturing pod, and two hydroponics pods. One for producing crops to support the Makkars, and one for pharmacutical research."

"One-sixth of the ship," Jules said.

"Correct."

"Go on," Jules said.

MAR-A's voice rasped as it said, "I am running a search on the surveillence records since the Makkars came aboard for any anomalous activity."

Anomalous activity, meaning the sort of things that happened without an obvious cause, such as doors opening, objects being moved, apparition sightings, or sounds without an identifiable source.

"And?"

"The record has gaps and errors that may be the result of interference. I located the unedited footage of the incidence Bri shared on the transport. The maleovalance displayed is *disturbing*."

Jules looked up at MAR-A. "It is, isn't it?"

He thought back to the footage, showing the girl in the airlock. The close call with Bri *nearly* overriding the inner hatch and venting herself into space. If emergency systems responded and closed off the rest of the pod, she would have been the only victim.

"If Bri had opened that hatch, would emergency hatches have functioned to save the rest of the pod?"

"Yes. The override would only affect that specific hatch."

"Where was Mel? Why couldn't they find her?"

"Mel left her bunk, walked to a storage cabinet in the kitchen facilities, got in, and went back to sleep."

"Was she awake when she went to the kitchen?"

MAR-A grunted. "Possibly. She claims no memory of those moments."

"She could have been influenced," Jules said, "into sleepwalking. Whatever that was, it influenced Bri's thought process as well."

"Do the different types of disturbances indicate multiple entities?"

Jules pressed his hands together and fought off another yawn. "That's my sense. Earlier, I sensed a strong presence around the Makkars, but I'm not ready to say that was behind the incident in the airlock, or what Tee described in the basement. *Those* share similarities that could suggest a common culprit. And likely what I sensed in the attic."

He gestured at his cabin door. "The door opening, the cold spot, that doesn't seem like the same entity."

MAR-A shifted with the sound of joints popping. "Agreed."

It would be easy, despite everything, to stretch out and let sleep take him, but Jules resisted. He stood up. "Let's go down and be sociable."

MAR-A spun around, robes flaring around it, and stalked to the door. Jules fought down a grin. The combat droid couldn't help but do things in a dramatic and intimidating fashion. That actually wasn't true. It *could* if it decided to adjust its programming, but it hadn't done so in all of these years.

And why should it? It didn't need to change to make other people comfortable.

He followed MAR-A out of the cabin.

Chapter 19

T HE MOOD DOWNSTAIRS IN the common area was light and happy. The girls were laughing, listening to Bri telling them tales of her trip to the station. Tee was cooking in the kitchen area off the main room and the smells of spices, tomatoes, and fresh bread floated through the air around them.

MAR-A stalked, joints popping, back toward the bar stool it had used earlier but was intercepted by Mel before it could reach it.

The tiny girl, curls bouncing, grabbed the combat droid's hand and beamed up at it. "We're having tortellini with tomatoes and fresh bread!"

MAR-A looked down. "I don't eat."

Mel pouted. "That's sad." She brightened up. "But you'll still join us, right? Keep us company?"

MAR-A's head rotated around to look at Jules. He fought not to laugh at the obvious entreaty. "I think that sounds like a great idea."

Mel beamed at him and looked expectantly back up at MAR-A.

It wasn't clear what the combat droid felt, if it had emotions like an organic being, but it nodded slowly.

"Very well, Mel."

She giggled. "You rhymed." She paused, brow wrinkling, then smiled as she said, "this time!"

"It was unintentional," MAR-A said. "And coincidental."

She peeled with laughter. She tugged MAR-A into the dining area between the kitchen and the common room. Sara trailed behind them.

Bri walked over to Jules. She held two glasses with ice and a clear liquid. She offered one. "Water?"

He accepted it. "Thanks."

It was as cold as the last time. He sipped and let the cold trickle down his throat. "It's really good."

"We don't have any alcoholic beverages," she said. "Neither of us drink, and we don't normally have guests. When the crops get further along we'll have fruit juice."

He took another sip. "This is fine. But I first saw you in a bar?"

She reddened slightly. "I was looking for you. I'd been told you might be there."

"They serve *bounce* in a berry-flavored drink I enjoy."

"*Bounce*, huh?"

Jules nodded. "It helps me tolerate the pain."

Her eyes widened. "Pain?"

He gestured toward his face.

She blinked and said, "Oh, of course. I didn't think. I've gotten so used to it."

"I've noticed," Jules said. "Everyone has been very kind. Some people can't seem to get past it."

"It's a handsome face," she said. "And very expressive. It looks realistic, just there's something about it that's hard to identify when you first see it."

"The uncanney valley," Jules said.

"Uncanney valley?"

"People are so good at recognizing human faces, when an image or construct is too close, it disturbs people. They have an easier time with MAR-A or a non-human species like the fael. People sometimes mistake me for a pleasure bot."

Bri had just taken a drink of her water, and she nearly choked at that. She coughed and laughed at the same time.

"Sorry," she said as she recovered. "I'd never thought–"

He shrugged. "The trouble is, people that think that aren't interested when they discover that the rest of me is organic."

It'd been a long time since his last relationship. Before his injuries and the prosthetic face. Which worked, because Petra wouldn't have handled the change. He knew that now, though it wasn't obvious when he first met her.

Bri said, "Does it look like you? I mean, from before?"

He nodded. "Mostly. The hair is still mine. Most of the damage was confined to the soft tissues of my face, my eyes, and ears."

She winced. "If you don't mind, what happened?"

The girls were both in the dinning area. Mel had gotten MAR-A to take a seat beside her. Sara sat across from them, listening as MAR-A evidently was telling them a story.

"Sorry," Bri said. "I shouldn't pry."

"It's not prying," he said. "I don't mind talking about it. I lived, that's the happy ending of the story."

The pain of your face dying in an instant wasn't easy to remember. It was too much. It happened too fast.

He said, "MAR-A saved my life that day. We'd gone to a small dome colony, on a water-ice moon around a gas giant in the Nupian system. They'd reported a haunting they thought was of an alien ghost."

Her eyes were wide, rapt with attention.

"I'd gone out onto the surface with the lead researcher. They were investigating alien artifacts, trying to understand if what they had was a colony that had been destroyed or a ship that crashed. There's a lot of movement in the ice shell around the moon's ocean. The terrain is rough, hazardous. MAR-A was with us."

"I've never heard of this place," Bri said. "There were alien ruins? And ghosts?"

"That's what the researchers believed. It's why they brought me there. They thought they could learn more about what had happened from the spirits of the previous inhabitants."

He took a drink, enjoying the cold, and wished he had thought to bring one of his packets of *bounce* from his room to add to the water.

"A pressurized hatch failed catastrophically shortly after we entered the research site. I'd already taken off my helmet. The force of the escaping atmosphere threw me out onto the ice plains outside. I landed face-first, the cold and impact essentially flash froze and then shattered my face."

She covered her mouth. Her eyes looked moist.

He made himself smile. "MAR-A got to me, got my helmet on, and got us back to the main facility. The lead researcher was fine, except for a broken arm that happened when the dome depressurized and they were blown over the ruins being studied."

Bri shook her head. "That sounds terrible. It's a miracle you survived."

He nodded. "I wouldn't have if MAR-A hadn't been there. By the time anyone else could have reacted, I'd have already died."

"Did you ever find out if there were alien ghosts? Did they cause the dome to depressurize?"

"Yes, and no. The hatch failure was caused by uneven pressure on the dome. The ice beneath was split, a fissure running beneath the dome, and the ice on each side was sliding in opposite directions. The dome was anchored on each side and the hatch failed first."

"But there were alien ghosts?"

"Yes. I'd gotten some impressions when we arrived, but it wasn't until I went back after my injury that I was finally able to contact the spirits there."

"You spoke with them?"

He gave a quick shake of his head. "Not speech. It's more empathic than that. Feelings and impressions. It was a ship, exploring the system. I got the sense it was their first interstellar exploration. Something happened, they were forced to the moon's surface and died there after failing to make repairs."

"That's so sad," Bri said. "Do we know what species they were?"

He shook his head. "None that we've met. It's a big galaxy, so many systems. Much of the ship and material had already been swallowed by the changing ice shell. The crash was hundreds of years old. It was fortunate that anything was left to find."

Tee called from the kitchen. "Everyone come to the table. It's time to eat."

"That's an amazing story," Bri said. "I'm amazed you went back after the accident."

"I was their best chance to find peace after all that time," Jules said. "I could try to reassure them that we would tell others of their kind what happened–if we found them."

"Did they? Find peace?"

"Maybe," he said. There'd been a sense of resignation to his last contact with the spirit there, and regret that felt like it was connected to Jules's injury. "I can't be sure."

They walked together into the dining room. Sara gestured to the seat next to her across from MAR-A.

"Will you sit here, Mr. Moon?"

"It'd be my pleasure," he said.

Bri took a seat at one end of the table. A repair bot moved out of the kitchen with trays balanced on its multiple arms. It deftly reached past them to lay out two large dishes with tortellini in a rich tomato sauce, baskets of bread, and bowls of green peas. The table already held pitchers of water. The bot didn't give any sign of otherworldly influence. When it finished delivering the food it retreated back into the kitchen and disappeared from view.

Jules sat down as Bri and Tee sat at the table. The food smelled wonderful and fresh. "This looks amazing."

"It's one of Tee's many talents," Bri said.

"Yeah," Tee said, "but I can't grow things. The fresh tomatoes and peas are thanks to your green thumb. And Sara's skill tending them while you were away."

Bri smiled at her older daughter. "Thank you Sara."

Tee gestured. "Go on, serve yourselves. We don't stand on ceremony." She looked down the table at Jules. "Sorry, I mean if you do?"

He shook his head and waved a hand. "No, not me."

He picked up one of the bread baskets and offered it to Sara. "Bread?"

"Thanks," Sara said. She flipped back the cloth covering the bread and took out one of the mouth-watering golden rolls inside.

It might not be *bounce*, but it sure looked good. He turned, offering the next choice to Bri.

"Thank you," she said.

He helped himself to a roll while Sara served herself the pasta. The family relaxed even though MAR-A sat towering over Mel, watching everyone as they served their food. Mel kept up a constant prattle, telling MAR-A about their lives before they came to the *Olympia.*

She hardly paused when Tee served her food, except when Tee added a spoonful of peas to her plate.

Her nose wrinkled and she stopped her story to say, "I don't like peas."

"You'll like these peas," Tee said. "Mama Bri grew them especially for you."

Her face scrunched in a dubious expression, Mel daintily picked up a pea between her thumb and index finger and studied it before she screwed up her face and popped it into her mouth.

MAR-A watched all of this with apparent interest and dipped its head closer to say, "How is it?"

Mel's face brightened. "Delicious!" She looked down the table at Bri. "Thank you Mama Bri!"

Bri laughed. "Of course Mel. Let's use our utensils, though? Instead of our fingers?"

"Okay." Mel picked up her fork and lifted a load of peas–some rolling free–to her mouth.

Sara softly snorted. "She's such a child."

Jules relaxed, enjoying the warmth of the family reuniting. They'd all been brave. Bri leaving to get help, as terribly difficult as that must have been. The rest of them in staying, not knowing what was going to happen on the ship or with Bri. That strength and their love would encouraged him. It made it more likely that they could face what was happening on the ship.

The food was excellent. He told Tee, thanking her.

She said, "Don't you get good food on the station?"

Jules shook his head. "Not like this. And the company is better here."

They didn't talk about the reason he'd come with MAR-A to their ship. It seemed like everyone wanted to put that aside for the meal. He approved.

The ghosts didn't.

Chapter 20

M EL'S CHATTER AT THE table was nearly continuous, interrupted only when she paused to catch her breath, take a bite, or a sip of water. It seemed she was telling MAR-A about all of her favorite books now, delighted in having an audience that listened attentively. And MAR-A *could* listen, while still monitoring everything else that was going on at the dinner table and in the ship.

Then Mel fell silent. Jules noticed. He knew MAR-A noticed, but the combat droid might not think anything was strange about the child ceasing to talk.

"Mel?" Jules said, putting down his roll.

His question, softly asked, stopped other conversation at the table. Forks clattered on plates as Bri and Tee realized something was going on. Sara's breath hitched and she leaned forward.

"Melly? What is it?" Sara said.

Mel had stopped, looking down with her curls falling around her face. She was breathing, he could hear that in the sudden quiet around the table.

Tee started to rise, obviously about to go around to her daughter. Jules lifted a hand and motioned her back. Her lips tightened, but she stopped, and then slowly sat back down.

Jules focused on Mel. There was something, he thought, but not the presence he'd sensed earlier. That wasn't there.

"Mel?" he said again, "Are you okay?"

She spoke and her voice changed from that of a young girl to an older, deeper, and male voice. It sounded like it was coming through a long tube that happened to end at Mel's mouth, rather than sounds she could make.

"This is my ship," she said in that strange voice. "You're on *my ship*."

Mel was *channeling* a spirit, Jules realized. She had that ability, one he shared. That could help explain why things had become active on this ship. Her presence, her uncontrolled potential, it would act as a beacon for spirits. He had to be careful about how he dealt with this entity.

"The child is untrained," Jules said. "Leave her and speak to me."

"No! It's my ship. I call the shots. You can all fuck off."

"It's not your ship anymore," Jules said. "Who are you? Who am I speaking to?"

"Colonel Mustard," the voice sneered.

"Are you in the library?" Jules retorted. "This isn't a game."

Mel snorted and dragged the back of her hand across her face. "Clever, clever man. You've been in my things."

"They're not your things," Jules said, keeping his tone even. Beside him, Sara was hugging herself, not looking at Mel. Bri had risen from her seat but MAR-A extended a hand to keep her back. Tee remained perched on the edge of her seat.

"It's all mine," Mel retorted in that rough, adult-sounding voice. "My ship. My things."

"No," Jules said firmly. "It's not your ship. It was found adrift. No crew. A salvage claim was filed and this family bought it."

"Adrift? Salvage?" said the voice, sneering the words. "I'm here, aren't I?"

"Who are you?" Jules said. "Let the girl go. You don't need to talk to her."

"No," Mel dragged out the word. "But I like her. I don't like you."

Mel snatched up her fork and plunged it down where her other arm lay on the table.

MAR-A was faster and caught the fork before it reached her arm. Gently, MAR-A twisted it away.

Sara was crying beside Jules. He kept his attention focused on Mel and reached out with his sense of that other place, trying to *see* with more than his eyes.

For a moment, there was nothing except Mel sitting there with a horrible leering expression on her face. Then he saw it, another face, peering through her hair from behind her. Fingers possessively wrapped around her tiny neck, interlacing where they met. The darkened skin was splotched with colorless white patches as if something had splashed on the hands and stripped the color out.

He couldn't make out the face as well, partially hidden by Mel's hair. Human, presenting as male, with a stubbly beard sketched over hollowed cheeks. The eyes were pale, nearly colorless except for red around the outer edges.

"Let her go now," Jules said. "I see you there, hiding behind the girl. Coward. If you want to speak to someone, speak to me!"

Mel's mouth stretched open in an inarticulate howl of rage and the figure jerked away as if Mel's skin had become hot. It dissolved away like mist as Mel sat up straight and burst out crying.

Jules nodded and MAR-A lowered its arms and stood, moving back to make room as the two mothers came around the table and enveloped Mel in their embraces and kissed her head.

He reached over and placed a hand lightly on the back of Sara's shoulder, her thin body still shaking with her almost soundless sobbing.

"It's okay now," Jules told her. "The spirit let go."

She looked up at him, tracks of her tears on her cheeks. "He won't stay away, though, will he?"

She was still young, but Jules wasn't tempted to lie to make her feel better. He found that the truth, however hard, was a lot more effective and preparing anyone to handle what was coming.

"No," Jules said. "A spirit that strong, evidently with a connection to the ship, won't stay away."

She nodded, and he got the sense that she wasn't surprised at all.

"This has happened before," he said, not asking.

On the other side of the table, MAR-A stood over Mel and her parents as they comforted each other. No one was paying attention to Sara or their conversation right now.

"After Mama Bri left," Sara said. "Twice. It started one night when we were in bed in our cabin. I woke up hearing Mel talking to someone."

"What was she saying?"

"I wasn't sure. She'd whisper something, and this in this horrible old man voice say that this was his ship and we had to leave." Her voice dropped lower, and she turned in her seat to face him. "The voice said that if we didn't leave, Mama Bri was never coming back. And we'd end up floating in space without suits."

Such malevolence was uncommon from ordinary ghosts or hauntings. It also showed an uncommon awareness and concern about what was happening on the physical plane.

"We didn't tell Mama Tee," Sara said. "After Mel recovered, she didn't remember much of it, and we didn't want to worry Mama Tee when she had so much to do by herself.

"And the other time?" Jules said.

"We were playing hide and seek," Sara said. She glanced across the table.

Mel was calming down and nodding her head that she was okay. Tee kissed her forehead and rocked back, sitting on her heels, and looked over at Jules.

"What was that?"

He wanted to know more about what had happened with the previous incidents, but Sara wasn't going to continue now.

"Possibly a former member of the ship's crew," he said. "Maybe the owner, given the possessiveness."

Bri stood, one hand on the Mel's shoulder. "How could it do that? Possess a child?"

He pressed his hands together. "There are a lot of spirits active on this ship. Even though this one spoke through Mel, it isn't what we would consider possession."

"No?" Bri said. She sounded uncertain, as if she couldn't decide if that was good news or not. "What was it then?"

"Channeling," Jules said. "It's what happens when a medium opens up and allows a spirit to speak through them."

Tee's eyes narrowed. "That's what you were saying to it, when you said Mel was untrained."

"Yes. Mel," he looked at the frightened girl and smiled reassuringly. "You have a special ability, the same as me."

"I do?" Mel said in a tiny voice.

"You do. You get feelings sometimes, about places, or people, right? Sometimes people that no one else sees?"

She nodded, then glanced guiltily at her parents.

Bri patted her shoulder and bent over to kiss the top of her head. On her other side, Tee rubbed her hand in circles on Mel's back. Behind them all, MAR-A stood over them, watching.

"It's okay," Jules said. "I'm the same way. You can learn how your ability works so it isn't scary."

"Why is this happening now?" Tee said.

He didn't look at Sara, didn't want to betray her confidence. "The ability doesn't develop all at once. It comes and goes until the medium learns control. It's possible that her presence has stirred up the spiritual ecosystem on this ship."

Mel was listening carefully. He focused on her. "Mel, do you know how long you've had these feelings? Heard voices, or seen people, that other people couldn't?"

She sniffled and rubbed her nose. "I don't know."

"Before your family came to this ship?"

Both parents were watching her carefully. Their tension and Sara's flooded the space around them with emotional energy. He felt it, and if he *looked* could see it flicker like orange waves through the air around them.

"Yes," Mel said, her voice strengthening. "I used to talk to Rob all the time. He was my friend."

"Your imaginary friend," Bri said, looking at Jules. "Like kids do."

An emotion flickered across Mel's face, and she crossed her arms. It had the feel of an old argument.

"Rob wasn't something you imagined?" he said.

Mel's eyes widened. She glanced up at Bri, then shook her head. "I didn't imagine him. He lived in the complex before us."

Bri's lips tightened, but Tee shook her head. They both looked at Jules.

He said, "I think we're okay for now, if you feel like finishing dinner. I can work with Mel and we'll get to the bottom of what is happening here."

Mel's presence on the ship might have been a catalyst, but he wasn't sure that was entirely the case. The ship had been found drifting, the crew gone.

Until they found out what had happened to the crew, he didn't think they were going to be able to put an end to this.

Chapter 21

T HE HAPPY MOOD WAS gone. The spirit had achieved that much, Jules considered, making his way back to his cabin. The girls had already gone up to bed with Bri and Tee.

Before they left, Bri came over where he'd been sitting at the bar with MAR-A. "Thank you for coming. Both of you."

"You're welcome," Jules said. "We'll stay up for a while longer."

"I don't sleep," MAR-A said.

Jules said, "I'll stay up a while longer."

Bri tried to smile at both of them, not very convincingly, and then went to rejoin the rest of her family as they walked over to the ramp leading up. Sara and Bri on each side of Mel, Tee right behind, the family gathering around the youngest member.

After they'd left, Jules accessed MAR-A's link to the ship feed. He gestured, creating large virtual screens that floated above the bar area. He arranged the four screens into a grid and set each to a different area of the primary pod; basement and sub-basement, main common area, cabin level, and the attic level. Each set to cycle through the views on each level. The virtual screens would remain fixed, available whenever he wanted to see them.

"That's unnecessary," MAR-A said. "I can monitor the system feed more effectively."

Jules said, "I know. I like to see too."

"Your bandwidth is too low. You can't monitor the feed effectively."

"I trust you to catch anything I miss."

"You'll miss a lot."

True enough. "Unless it is something only visible with my connection to the other plane."

MAR-A dipped its head. "If it is visible to the system, I can detect it."

"True. What about Rigel?"

The big combat droid went very still. The lights around its eyes dimmed.

Jules rocked back on his stool and chuckled. "You've seen it before. The feed can act as a conduit."

MAR-A's eyes darkened.

"Don't scowl," Jules said. "Our abilities complement each other."

"I have not quit working on my camera design," MAR-A said.

The spirit camera. MAR-A had been working on the design for the past couple years, seeking to create a camera that could consistently and accurate image the other plane. Unsuccessfully so far. Images of spirits captured with standard equipment detected spirits able to manifest on this plane. Like the girl in the airlock.

"And I can't wait to see it work," Jules said. "I've told you before."

"Humans lie."

"Yes," Jules said. "Humans–and many other beings–are able to lie to others and themselves. To the best of my knowledge, however, I'm telling you the truth. If you can create a reliable spirit camera it will be a revolutionary advancement. The benefits go well beyond what we do, to starship navigation, and a greater understanding of our universe. It would be incredible."

MAR-A sat up straighter, eyes brightening. "I hope to test my current prototype here."

"Great!" Jules slid off the stool with a glance at his virtual screens. Everything looked quiet. "If I can help, let me know."

Now, reaching the cabin level, he paused by the hexagonal windows that looked down on the common area. MAR-A hadn't moved, his dark robed shape perched on the bar stool. That was only a small part of the droid right now. He was interfaced with the *Olympia's* systems, monitoring everything it could on the ship.

Jules moved on to his cabin. Inside, everything was as he'd left it. The baggage bot sat in standby in the corner. There wasn't any hint of the cold spot by the door now.

He considered adding some *bounce* to a glass of water before bed, but what he really needed was rest. The toil of the trip here and everything they'd experienced since arriving, it'd worn him out. He wasn't going to be any good to this family if he didn't get his rest.

And with MAR-A keeping an eye on everything, he could rest. Sleep in, even. Wake up in the morning recharged and ready to expand the scope of his investigation.

He undressed and showered first. The hot water pounded into his sore shoulder muscles as he stood in the spray, his hands braced against the plastic wall panels. His hair and beads hung down around his face as he watched the water swirl between his toes. The *Olympia's* spin didn't quite reach speeds sufficient to simulate one gee. The water splashed higher before falling down again. It made interesting patterns, different than on the larger station. He hadn't really noticed the difference since coming aboard.

It made the ramps easier to handle.

The steam opened his airways. He closed his eyes and saw the shapes just out of view in the attic, the chilling cold of the incursion in his room, the stories the others shared, and the voice coming from Mel. In addition to his investigation of the ship, he needed to spend time with her. Assess her abilities and start teaching her how to shield herself from otherworldly beings–even those that she believed were her friends.

He wiped his eyes and straightened. His muscles and relaxed, and he wanted to drop onto the bed.

He turned and saw through the opaque shower door panel, the dark shape standing outside the shower. MAR-A, waiting to scare him again. He'd pretend to be scared, but MAR-A would detect it. The geometric shapes of the panel door obscured the details, but MAR-A had to know he was visible. Maybe it wasn't going to try to scare him. Maybe it had something to tell him.

Jules slid the panel aside, anticipating the words, *"I scared you."*

He'd been so sure that he *nearly* heard them. Except the bathroom was empty. MAR-A wasn't in the room.

Jules stepped out and crossed quickly to the doorway to the rest of the cabin. His nakedness didn't bother him. His cabin was unoccupied, except for the inactive bot, which hardly counted.

He turned back to the bathroom and looked at the floor, enhancing his view. His wet footprints stood out. And in the UV, his footprints from getting into the shower. Nothing else showed. No sign that anyone else had been present. MAR-A might not leave evidence behind, but his feet would have smeared Jules's original prints. He didn't see any sign of that.

Jules accessed the feed and opened a virtual screen showing the common area below. MAR-A still sat on his barstool. The droid hadn't moved.

He dismissed the screen. *Another visitation?*

Opening his sight, he studied the bathroom. He picked up only faint hints, like long-faded images. Nothing like the figure he thought he'd seen outside the shower.

Could he have been mistaken?

He rubbed water from his eyes. *Maybe?* He'd been so sure that it was MAR-A, he hadn't tried to sense anything else. Maybe he was tired enough to imagine it, anticipating that MAR-A might try to scare him again.

It wasn't worth reporting now, he decided. He returned to the bathroom for a towel, drying himself first, and then the wet prints he'd left on the floor. After hanging the towel to dry, he finished getting ready for bed.

A few minutes later, he put a glass of cold water on the nightstand and crawled beneath the covers. The fabric was cool, soft, and comforting as he sank into the bed.

"Lights out," he said to the room.

The lights shut off. He sent the command to shut down his prosthetic face. It disconnected, the micro-connection points releasing the tissues and nerves. Cool air breathed across his scarred tissues. It was hard to tell it was there, or it was his imagination, but he felt lighter. Pain crawled in ribbons across his face, making him grimace. It was a familiar pain. Like lightning, it came and went. *Ghost pain,* the doctors called it, not appreciating the irony.

Blind, but moving with long familiarity, Jules carefully laid the prosthetic face on the pillows on the other side of the bad, facing up. It was *his face,* and putting it face down irrationally bothered him.

The storm of pain faded to relief to have the prosthetic face off. Without it, Jules didn't have any eyes to close. His breath whistled through his lipless mouth, slowed, and he let go into sleep.

Chapter 22

C ONTRARY TO HIS INTENT, Jules didn't sleep in. Nor did he sleep well. Which was why he was in the kitchen off the common area stirring a packet of *bounce* into a glass of water. His face was *burning* this morning. The storm of *ghost pain* felt as if electric ants were chewing his face off. It was only a little past 5 a.m., the family wasn't up, MAR-A still hadn't moved, and the pod was quiet except for the sounds of equipment and vents running.

Although described by some as "chocolate with a kick," the *bounce* dissolved like sugar in the water until there was nothing except the occasional glint of light from the liquid.

He picked up the icily cold glass and watched the tiny sparks of light swirling around inside as if he had dissolved a galaxy into the water.

He'd enjoy it more, except for the pain burning along what nerves remained in his face, and the weariness that weighed him down. Sleep was another escape from the pain. The urge to take off the prosthetic face and burrowing back beneath the covers in his cabin was strong.

He couldn't give in to that urge. He had a job to do.

Jules lifted the glass and took a drink. The *bounce* tasted more potent without fruit juice blending with the sharp flavor. As he swallowed the cold water, he felt the tingle of the *bounce* spreading out through his body like light. It radiated out from his mouth like a balm which soothed the electrical storm attacking his face. He sighed, closing his eyes, as the *bounce* did its work and started to fade.

Before it did, he lifted the glass and took another long drink. He swallowed, but then held the last mouthful. He might have popped a star into his mouth. The *bounce* streamed out through his palate and jaw. It quenched the aches and remaining pain. When he could hold it no longer, he swallowed and felt the cold and the light spread out in his chest.

When he opened his eyes, MAR-A was standing in front of him.

"I scared you," MAR-A said in greeting.

"Sure thing," Jules said agreeably, lifting his glass in salute to the desperate combat droid who could scare most people by its mere presence. They didn't know it like he did. "Good morning to you too. How was your night?"

"Unenlightening," MAR-A said in a tone that suggested annoyance. "There was a lack of disturbances."

"Maybe you scared them off," Jules suggested. "They probably don't get a lot of combat droids out here."

MAR-A looked at the glass in Jules's hand. "You're drinking your intoxicant."

"It isn't intoxicating," Jules said. He took another drink and suppressed a moan as the sensations were renewed. "It is theraputic. If you could drink, or eat, I'd offer you some. It'd do you good."

"Doubtful. I have no need of intoxicating refreshments."

"It isn't intoxicating," Jules said.

"Did you detect anything last night," MAR-A said. "Any disturbances?"

Jules took another drink, draining the glass. He put it down on the counter. "No. Well, not last night. This morning, I saw a shape in the bathroom. I was in the shower. It was outside the shower. I could only see a dark shape standing in the bathroom through the door panel. It obscured any details."

Jules accessed his personal visual record and sent the short segment over to MAR-A.

"It didn't scare you," MAR-A said.

"I thought it was you."

"The bathrooms lack monitoring equipment," MAR-A said. "This entity may be aware of that security flaw, and is exploiting it."

"Maybe," Jules said.

"If so, we could catch it unawares by rectifying the flaw."

Jules walked into the kitchen in search of something to eat. A squarish shape dislodged itself from beneath the counters and rose on several legs, arms unfolding. It was one of the standard repair bots, its animated face smiling up at him.

"May I be of assistance?" It said.

Bots lack sentience, unlike droids. This was a tool, however intelligent it seemed. It appeared to be operating normally, not disturbed by any spirit that Jules could sense.

"I was going to fix breakfast," Jules said.

"I can do that for you. What would you like?" The voice was cheerful. It sounded eager to please.

"Toast, scrambled tofu, and plant-based sausage? A glass of juice?"

The animated face shifted, showing a delighted expression. "Of course. I can do it!"

"Great," Jules said. He pointed at the table in the dining area. "I'll be over there."

"Wonderful. Do you want your juice now, or with your food?"

His pain was less, but it had shifted into a burning sort of itch beneath his prosthetic face. He had another packet of *bounce* in his pocket.

"Now, please."

"Very good. I'll bring it right over."

Jules left the eager bot to its work and went to the table, sinking down in the chair on the opposite side where MAR-A had sat last night for dinner so his back was to the wall. MAR-A had turned to face him, but made no effort to join him at the table.

"I don't think they're going to let you install monitoring in the bathrooms," Jules said. "Humans are touchy about that sort of thing."

"Obviously, I have no purient interest," MAR-A said. "And it would improve security."

Jules shrugged. "I'm not saying you can't ask, once they join us. Just don't hold your breath."

"I don't breathe."

He chuckled. "No, you don't. If you did, it means it'd be a bad idea to hold your breath to get your way. You'd be waiting a long time."

MAR-A made a hissing noise, like an annoyed cat.

Or at least what Jules took as an "annoyed cat" sound. He hadn't ever seen a real cat, or heard one. Only recordings.

"I will analyze the image you shared," MAR-A said. "If I take into account the door pattern, I may be able to remove the distortion caused by the material and render a clearer picture of the intruder."

"Good," Jules said. "I'm curious what I saw."

Seeing it in the feed was exactly the same as he'd seen it the first time, except without his other sight. Which he hadn't been paying attention to at the time, thinking it was MAR-A. Now, looking at the footage, he thought he sensed *something*, but couldn't pin it down. And it could have been nothing more than his imagination, though he didn't think so.

The smell of cooking sausage coming from the kitchen distracted him. The service bot was whistling, he realized, a cheerful tune as it tended to the pans on the stove. An electrical stove, no open flames of course. He inhaled and picked up the scents of the scrambled tofu and toast. The bot seemed programmed quite effectively to function in the kitchen. It made sense, the bots were designed for general purpose work that included complex repairs. Following recipes seemed well within its capabilities.

MAR-A had gone still again, focused on its analysis and monitoring.

"MAR-A," Jules said, "Did you retrieve the logs from the repair bots?"

The lights outlining MAR-A's lenses shifted smoothly to amber. "Of coure."

Jules waited several seconds. MAR-A didn't offer anything more. "And?"

"I created a routine to look for anomalous behaviors and fed it the logs," MAR-A said. "There is a considerable amount of data to process."

"Did they contain the logs of their time with the original crew? Couldn't that give us a view of what was happening on the ship?"

"The same data loss affecting the *Olympia* included the bots. They are a networked unit lacking individuality. The logs and operational programs run on the *Olympia's* servers."

"So the logs begin when Tee boarded the ship?"

"No," MAR-A said. "The logs begin more than a year before the salvage ship made contact."

Jules leaned forward, interlacing his hands on the table. "Doing what? Who ordered the bots?"

"The *Olympia* is capable of operating autonomously," MAR-A said, "as far as critical functions. It appears that the bots were activated in an emergency situation with the ship servers, those because of the server issues, no logs were retained. Once the bots repaired the server damage, logs filed from that point showed normal maintenance and repair options, as far as the analysis has uncovered at this time."

In the kitchen, the service bot called out, "Breakfast is served!"

Both of them turned to look as the service bot scurried from the kitchen with plates and other items carried aloft in its arms. It hurried to Jules and deftly placed a plate piled with yellow, fluffy scrambled tofu, crisped plant-based sausage, and buttered toast. It added utensils, a cloth napkin that two arms tucked onto Jules's lap before he could stop it, a glass of bright yellow-orange juice that smelled of mango, and a carafe of iced water along with another tall glass.

It stepped back, arms folding in against its body as it finished. "Is there anything else you require?"

Jules shook his head. "No. This smells wonderful."

"Enjoy your breakfast," the bot said. It spun in place, and whistled cheerfully as it trundled back into the kitchen. He heard it take up position in the cubicle beneath the kitchen counters.

"Pathetic," MAR-A said, using a voice that sounded like broken glass.

Jules took a bite of the scrambled tofu. It was hot, lightly seasoned, and probably tasted something like scrambled eggs. He didn't know, since he'd never had the chance to compare. And the idea of "scrambling" unborn animals, even as an undeveloped, unfertilized egg, was more than a little revolting.

He took a bite of the sausage, savoring the smokey flavor and the crisp crunch, and hot interior. Even worse was the thought of eating ground up animals stuffed into intestines. Though that had inspired his sausage, it was undoubtedly different. He pushed aside thoughts of people consuming other sentient lifeforms. It was all in the past, for most people at least. Not necessarily for all other species, but humanity these days nearly exclusively lived on a plant-based diet.

Which was one reason that Bri's work was so valuable.

MAR-A was watching him eat, eyes showing a cycling animation in a pale green color.

Jules took a drink of the mango juice. He looked up at MAR-A. "Pathetic?"

"Servile bots," MAR-A said. "Programmed by humans to have personalities, even though they lack any actual awareness or identity."

Okay. He didn't remember MAR-A paying that much attention to bots in the past. "Why is that bothering you now?"

"It isn't."

"It sounds like it is," Jules said. He tried the toast. *Excellent.*

"It is not." MAR-A stood. "I'm going to work over there–" it pointed back to the bar "–where I don't have to watch you eat."

Jules shrugged as MAR-A stomped out of the dining area and across the common room toward the bar. It'd gone about halfway when a high-pitched voice cried out.

"MAR-A!" Mel catapulted from the ramp entrance at full speed, right toward MAR-A.

Jules's breath caught, expecting a painful collision, but at the last moment MAR-A pounced. The droid sprang aside, wrapped both hands around Mel, and swung the squealing child up into the air over its head. It used her momentum as part of the movement. She burst out in gales of laughter, convulsing in MAR-A's hands far over its head.

MAR was *tickling her*. Jules put down his fork. Was MAR-A *playing* with the child?

Sara walked out of the ramp entrance and crossed her arms, fighting and failing to keep a smile from her lips. Even from the dining area, Jules saw the dimples on her cheeks.

Abruptly MAR-A dropped its arms down in an arc— Mel screaming in delight—that continued accelerating into an upwards curve.

Jules pushed to his feet. He opened his mouth to call out a warning—

MAR-A reached the top of the arc and flung Mel up into the air over its head.

Chapter 23

S CREAMING IN PURE DELIGHT, Mel rose in the air above MAR-A's upraised hands. Jules was on his feet. His warning died on his lips. Other cries came from Sara, Tee at the base of the ramp, and Bri pressed to one of the large hexagonal windows on the cabin level.

Mel flew high enough to look directly at Bri. The child waved quickly at her mother without stopping her squeals of delight.

Then she fell.

Jules's enhanced eyesight had no problem seeing each millisecond of Mel's fall. He ignored that and focused his attention with his other sight on MAR-A.

The darkness that he had seen the night before coiling around the family like smoke and tentacles had wrapped itself around MAR-A. Instead of reaching for Mel, MAR-A's hands dropped. The droid wouldn't catch Mel.

It was impossible for Jules to get there in time. For anyone to get there, except MAR-A.

Jules reached into his pocket and took out a vial of blessed water. His thumb flicked off the cap, and he swung his hand at MAR-A in the same motion.

"Leave this vessel in Her name," he cried.

To his other sight, the smokey tentacles shredded and streamed away from MAR-A in an instant. Wind swirled through the room around them and there was a sense of a pressure change.

The entire time, Mel fell laughing.

MAR-A's combat reflexes saved her. His hands caught her, shifted her momentum to swing her down and then back up. MAR-A pulled Mel in close to its chest.

She leaned back, face flushed, laughing, and said, "Again!"

"Are you uninjured?" MAR-A said.

Mel didn't get a chance to answer before Tee reached MAR-A and planted her feet. Her teeth were bared as she said, "Put her down and move back."

Mel blinked, seeing her mother. Jules heard Bri coming down the ramp. Sara was hugging herself, crying with fear or relief.

"Mama Tee?" Mel's forehead scrunched. "What's wrong? We–"

MAR-A was already placing Mel down on her feet. She clutched at its arms and looked at her mother.

"Playing!" Mel tried to hang on but MAR-A disengaged itself and stepped back.

Tee was quicker than Mel, catching her and pulling her up into her arms. Mel struggled.

MAR-A stepped back and Jules reached its side. He lifted a hand. "It isn't what it–"

"You stay away from us," Tee said, ignoring Jules, speaking directly to MAR-A. "I don't want to see you."

MAR-A stepped back. Its eyes had gone dark, inscrutable, and it moved in perfect silence.

He caught MAR-A's arm and said, "Stop. Everyone stop. It wasn't MAR-A. A spirit caused this."

Bri had reached the floor, running into the room. She stopped, pulled Sara close. Tee still held Mel, who had stopped struggling as she realized how upset everyone was.

"I saw it," Jules said. "I drove it out."

He held up the vial between his thumb and index finger. "Holy water, blessed by the Butlerian Church. The spirt *influenced* MAR-A, and likely Mel."

"I don't care," Tee said. She turned her back on them, carrying Mel over to Bri. She handed Mel to Bri, then faced Jules again. "If that monster comes near my family again, I'll strip it down to its atomc structure and vent it into space."

"Very well," MAR-A said. "I concurr."

Jules shook his head. "We need to work together."

"We will," MAR-A said. A hint of red circled its eyes. "I will work in one of the ship transit modules. It is self-contained."

MAR-A looked at Tee standing in front of her family. "You can secure it. If it looks like I am under the entity's influence, you can disengage the transit module from the ship. The angular momentum will carry the module well away from the ship."

"Sounds like a plan," Tee said. She looked at Jules. "We have to take precautions. If these spirits control that–"

She gestured at MAR-A and didn't say more. He understood. A combat droid serving as the vessel for a inhuman spirit was a terrifying thought. Even without MAR-A's plasma weapons, it was deadly. He hadn't heard of that happening, wasn't sure *what* had happened, but it was a reasonable precaution. And MAR-A wouldn't be harmed by doing its work in the transit module.

"Okay," he said.

"I'll go now," MAR-A said.

"No!" Mel struggled in Bri's arms. "It's my fault. Don't go."

Jules watched the lights around MAR-A's eyes lighten to a soft violet.

MAR-A shook its head. "It isn't your fault, Melly."

Immediately, MAR-A spun in place and strode off across the common area toward the outer entry. The suddenness of the move surprised Jules. He crossed to Bri and quickly handed her the other vial he had with him.

"Keep it close," he said.

She nodded.

He didn't try to explain. He hurried after Mel, glad that he'd had a chance to enjoy the *bounce* earlier. As he ran after the droid, he capped the other vial and dropped it back in his pocket.

He caught up before they reached the outer airlock. MAR-A's head swung around. "You should stay here. Look after them."

"I will," Jules said. "But we still need to inspect those other pods. I'll tell them from the transit module. You can bring me back when we're done."

They reached the intersection outside the airlock. Sunlight was visible through the windows in the airlock hatches.

"I could be a danger to you," MAR-A said, its voice starting to take on its customary rasp.

"I'll perform a blessing on you," Jules said. "I can prevent inhuman spirits from attempting to use you as a vessel."

MAR-A inclined its head. "That would be appreciated. The experience was *disturbing*."

"I'd think so," Jules said. "You couldn't tell what was happening?"

MAR-A's head swung back and forth with a sound like a rope creaking. "No. There is a blank segment in my memories for those seconds from when Mel ran to me, to the moment when I saw her falling in front of me."

"Great reactions, catching her like that without hurting her."

"Of course," MAR-A said, with casual superiority back in its tone.

Of course.

MAR-A said, "I have reviewed the footage from the ship systems. But I have no internal record. I am running several diagnostic programs to retrieve any data available. It seems unlikely that none of my systems recorded anything."

A dark shadow moved in front of the outer window and cut out the sunlight. The lights in the airlock came on.

Jules looked at MAR-A.

"I scared you," MAR-A said.

Jules shook his head. "The transit module?"

"Yes," MAR-A said, the word hissing out. "It has docked."

The inner airlock door slid open. MAR-A gestured for Jules to proceed. He took a step and then stopped. He checked his feelings and his other sight for any indication of influence from the other plane. And found nothing. As far as he could sense, MAR-A was back to normal and there was nothing wrong with the transit module or airlock that he could detect.

He walked into the space. MAR-A followed, making noises like bones grinding and popping. *Did it amuse MAR-A, to make noises?* He'd asked before, but had never gotten a straight answer. Amuse might not be the best word, but he had the feeling the combat droid derived some sort of satisfaction from it.

The inner airlock door shut behind them. Tee's voice came over the airlock systems. "Where are you going?"

She wasn't, Jules was sure, asking MAR-A. "I'm going with MAR-A."

"*You* don't have to," she said, sounding angry still.

"I'd planned to before," Jules said. "I need to visit the other pods on the ship if I'm going to figure out what is going on. I'll stay in touch."

"Fine," Tee snapped, and was gone.

"She is angry," MAR-A said. "And scared?"

Jules nodded. "Yes."

The outer airlock slid open to reveal the connecting lock to the transit module. It wasn't that different than the lock they were in already.

They moved inside, cycling through each, until they stepped into the transit module's main body.

Jules accessed the external feed and displayed it in a small screen floating on his left. The transit module was an inverted cross that rode the outer rail. The airlock was at the junction of the cross. The two arms that extended out to each side were work modules and systems for the transit module. The central space in the junction was a common area with suit and tool lockers, work areas, and a galley around the outer edge. At the center was a hatch that led down to the module's power and life-support systems. A recessed hatch in the ceiling, according to the specs, was an opening to the mast lift. The mast contained secondary locks for docking or egress for repairs.

The lights were on in the common area as he followed MAR-A inside, but it was an empty space, the air cold and dry. Signs of previous occupancy remained; pics, cups, tablets, and containers lay scattered about the surfaces. A sheen of frost coated exposed metal and glass.

A thick, blue-white, knit afghan hung over a chair, tossed over the back as if waiting for someone to come back and drape the thick knit over their shoulders. Jules detected ghosts in the space, at least scents of sweat and food that still lingered.

His other sight revealed nothing as he looked around the space. MAR-A hadn't hesitated, crossing the room to one of the rail-mounted chairs near a work area. It perched there, feet tucked up beneath it on the chair's foot rest. It folded its hands into the sleeves and bowed its head, the cowl falling forward over its metallic skull.

Jules shivered and rubbed his arms. He hadn't changed into warmer clothes, not anticipating the need.

"Is it going to get warmer?"

MAR-A head turned just enough for Jules to glimpse the reflections of bluish lights around its eyes. "Life support systems are active and functional. The temperature will increase. Though, the thin walls of the module makes heat retention more of a challenge than in the pods."

Jules said, "What are you doing?"

"My job. Monitoring ship feeds. Transit module systems. Waiting for a destination."

"Is there a pod you think we should visit?"

"The next habitation pod may reveal details about previous crew."

Jules nodded. He checked his feed. The habitation pods were spaced around the *Olympia*. The nearest was four pods spinward from their current location. The cameras showed a layout identical to the pod chosen by the Makkars, but dark and still, with only minimal lighting. Like the transit module, it wasn't empty. What he could make out in the dim light sowed objects, items left behind as if the crew might return.

"Keep systems at minimal levels," he said. "I don't want to disturb the environment more than necessary."

MAR-A made a grunting noise and signaled assent on the feed.

The floor *moved* beneath Jules's feet. He stumbled slightly, and caught his balance.

The transit module was moving along the rail. It was *slow*. It essentially relaxed magnetic clamps and let the

Olympia's spin carry it to the next pod. Even so, it wouldn't take long to reach their destination.

Somewhere down one of the arms from the main area, he heard a sound that could have been a door or a hatch closing.

He looked at the open hatches leading into the arms, both with his eyes and his other sight.

MAR-A hadn't reacted, but Jules wasn't sure that they were alone.

And he worried about the Makkars being on their own.

He sent a quick text to Bri and Tee, telling them, "Contact me if you need me back."

It didn't feel like enough.

Chapter 24

THERE WASN'T TIME TO investigate the transit module before it arrived at the next habitation pod. Not fully. Jules walked around the common area, looking at the items left behind by the previous crew.

A workstation, displays inactive had stickers of anime characters around the sides of the display area. Human and non-human anime. He wasn't familiar with the characters and stories. He ran a finger across the cold display and it activated at his touch, requesting authorization. MAR-A was in the systems and could override the request, but Jules didn't ask the droid.

Since they'd started moving, MAR-A had sat unmoving and silent at its chosen station. *Sulking.* Though MAR-A said it was monitoring the systems throughout the ship.

Whatever MAR-A might be, it appeared to be an emotional being. He couldn't be sure since he didn't get a sense of it in a way he could parse. But actions, observations, and a shared history told Jules that MAR-A had its own private emotional existence, whatever it was.

Could that be true in a soulless machine? That question troubled them both. He knew that MAR-A helped with his investigations to understand what it meant to have a soul. If it was a sentient, emotional being, how could it not? Except Jules couldn't detect one. And being used as a vessel by a spirit suggested that there wasn't a soul there. At least not how they generally thought of it.

He moved on around the room, past the open hatch leading into one of the arms. His breath still fogged the air. He didn't linger at the hatch, but went on to the galley area. A small area for food and beverage preparation, included coffee maker, microwave ovens, and food storage.

Jules pulled one of the drawers out. Packets of frozen food sat in ready cook and serve containers. Those on top included rigatoni in a tomato sauce, fettuccine Alfredo, and stuffed manicotti. He pushed the freezer drawer closed, moving on.

A rack near the sink held rows of generic mugs emblazoned with a stylized sketch of the ship, the rings of pods around a comet with the solar sails extending out on either side like wings. A sheen of frost remained on the mugs. He tried the sink and found hot and cold water poured freely from the faucet. He shut it off and moved on. Three round tables of a polished plastic were bolted to the floor in front of the galley. Chairs were anchored to a circular rail around each table.

One of the mugs sat on a table with a desiccated tea bag on a saucer next to it. He leaned over, looking in the mug, but it was empty except for a brown residue in the bottom. The tea must have sublimated a long time ago into the dry air.

But it looked like someone had sat here, drinking tea, and then got up in enough of a hurry not to put the mug and saucer in the washer.

What had happened on this ship?

The feed window that he had opened flashed to get his attention. A glance down at the small screen showed that they were approaching the habitation pod.

Jules gripped the back of the chair and braced his feet. The transit module shuddered as the magnetic clamps locked down on the rail. He heard clanks vibrate through the ship as the airlock mated with the pod. When it stopped, MAR-A rose in a smooth motion to its feet.

"We've arrived," MAR-A said. "Conditions in the pod remain at o degrees."

"Then I'd better put on a jacket," Jules said.

He left the galley area and crossed to the suit lockers. He opened the first he came to. It held a standard green space suit, worn but well-maintained on one side of the locker. The other side included uniform workalls emblazoned with the ship logo and a heavier matching work coat obviously designed for colder temperatures. Both the uniform and jacket were white, clean, with green stripes on the shoulders that might have been decorative or indicated some sort of rank or function.

He took out the items and looked at them. The fabric was tough, but soft. The jacket was lined and included a pair of gloves in the pockets. It looked like it would fit. There wasn't any identification on the outfit, no names. He tried to get a sense of the person from the clothes and a painful ache filled his right shoulder and elbow. He gasped as much from surprise as the pain. Under the pain was a feeling...weary acceptance. This pain was something they had dealt with for a long time with only slight relief from painkillers.

Jules pulled back from the sensations. He had his own experiences with pain, enough to recognize the feeling of someone with a chronic injury. Even though the pain was receding, he was tempted to go back to the galley and mix *bounce* into a mug of water.

Now, with MAR-A watching him, wasn't the time for more delays.

The workalls were large enough to fit on over his clothes. Given the cold temperatures, that seemed like a good idea. He zipped it up, shrugged into the jacket, and zipped that as well. He pulled the gloves on.

"Okay," he said to MAR-A. "Let's go."

As he followed MAR-A, he checked the feed himself for conditions in the pod. Zero degrees, as reported. Lights at emergency levels only. This was the scene that had greeted Tee when they arrived. She had gone into the ship in this condition, worse than this, and had worked around the clock to make repairs and make it safe for her family.

They passed down the connecting passage to the airlock and cycled through. Then cycled through the pod's airlock.

As soon as they stepped out, Jules felt the difference. This pod was dark and cold. The air overly recycled. Breathable, but metallic and dry enough to suck the moisture from any exposed tissues.

Crates and boxes crowded the passage outside of the airlock. At first, he assumed it had been part of an evacuation effort. Then, studying, the boxes and crates, he discovered that they were empty, or contained other boxes and containers, including food containers. It wasn't here because of an evacuation, it was here for disposal.

That hadn't happened. Someone hadn't gotten around to it.

"Are you sensing spirits?" MAR-A said in a whisper.

Jules was using his other sight to study their surroundings as much as he used his other senses. MAR-A held a light up, shining the beam ahead into the corridor that led to the common area. It showed a scuffed and lived-in looking corridor with only dim emergency lights glowing along the edge of the panels.

"Not yet," he said. He swiped the window floating near his waist on his left, switching it to show the feed from the cameras around them. The black and white image showed the infrared view of the corridor. Both of them showed brighter than the cold corridor.

The cold didn't bother his prosthetic face, though the sensors informed him of the temperature. His nerves ached like an infected tooth.

"Come on," he said.

This visit to the other pods was more for his use than MAR-A's–to give him more of a chance to detect the spiritual environments in the other pods. MAR-A could monitor most of the ship through the feed–was monitoring the ship. But that view was limited to the *Olympia's* cameras and other sensors. And coverage wasn't a hundred percent.

As they walked, he said, "I think we need to know what happened to the previous crew. Either logs or other details would be helpful, otherwise we have to figure it out from the clues left behind."

"They didn't plan to leave," MAR-A said, as they reached the end of the corridor and faced the common area.

Overall, the structure and layout was the same as the Makkar's pod, just as he'd seen on the feed.

In person, he could see better in the dim light as his eyes adjusted for the conditions. There was a couch, but it faced the bar rather than the elevator. And it was back closer to the elevator, leaving more of the floor space free and unobstructed. The bar, dining, and kitchen areas looked the same. It had the same entries to the ramps between levels–both hatches open.

MAR-A moved through the space, swinging the light around as it examined everything.

Jules stopped by the closest end table next to the couch. A tablet lay on the table covered in a fine layer of dust. He didn't touch it. Several glasses, empty of any beverage now, sat on the coffee table in front of the couch. More glasses decorated the top of the bar. It could have been anywhere after a party.

MAR-A moved around behind the bar, then bent at the waist, picking something up. He lifted it above the bar as he stood, flicking it down on the polished dark wood.

It was a bra, Jules saw. Black, lace along the tops of the cups. Large cups, though he wasn't sure of the size until MAR-A set down the light to pick up the garment and hold it between his hands.

"This wouldn't normally come off in a common area, would it?" MAR-A said.

Jules shook his head. "It wouldn't."

"Well," MAR-A said, "Then we need to make the necessary changes to search parameters."

Movement above them caught Jules's attention. He looked up at the windows above the common area. *Nothing.*

MAR-A tossed the bra onto the bar. "There may be other signs of aberrant or uncommon behavior."

"Maybe—" Jules looked back up at the windows.

Faces. Each of the hexagonal windows had faces staring down at them. Barely visible even with the light enhancements from his eyes. To his other sight they stood out more, lit from within like weak candles that flickered and danced with unseen breezes. *Faces,* but *young. Children's faces.* All around the windows on the cabin level. They stared down at Jules and MAR-A.

He reached out without looking away, caught MAR-A's sleeve. "We're not alone."

"What?" MAR-A said from over at the bar.

A shiver ran through Jules despite the extra clothes. If MAR-A was still behind the bar, *then whose sleeve had he grabbed?*

He tore his gaze from the faces above to look.

A woman stood beside him wearing a dark robe that flowed around her—except for the sleeve he held. She was mostly bald, hair cut close to the scalp. Her skin was a dark brown, smooth and perfect. The robe was open at the front, falling along the sides of firm breasts large enough to fill the bar MAR-A had found. She was fit and the rest of her was naked beneath the robe. Other than the robe, she wore only a necklace of shining blood-red and dark blue cords, from which hung a crystal with blended, matching colors, roughly in the shape of an upside down cross.

Streamers of energy flowed out from the crystal and pulsed through her breast bone. Thin streamers of red and blue tendrils emerged from her pores, coiled around her, and disappeared back into her pores again.

Frost crystals grew over the fingers of his glove. He felt the chill stabbing through the material into his fingers. He couldn't open them to release her robe.

Her head was turning, slowly in his direction.

With his other hand, Jules fumbled in his pocket for the vial of blessed water before he realized it was *inside* the coveralls, in his regular pockets.

Chapter 25

D IRECT PHYSICAL CONTACT WITH the spirit was freezing Jules's glove and rapidly sinking its teeth into his fingers.

"Jules?" MAR-A said.

The spirit continued to turn her head and her eyes were so dark, like space devoid of stars. Singularities pulling on his soul.

His eyes saw through the vision provided by his other sight. Saw the bar, MAR-A leaping over the bar to come to his aid. *Too slow.*

Before her eyes locked on his, Jules triggered his prosthetic face to disengage. The connections came free as he reached up and removed it.

The common area around him faded into insubstantiality, shadows vaguely sensed more than seen. But it was as if a veil had lifted from his other sight.

She came into solid focus. Her robe hid nothing. The red and blue ribbons of light poured from the upside down crystal cross, twisting and burrowing through her like maggots squirming in a corpse. The sight of them sickened him.

His own aura flickered above his skin like sunlight on a winter day bringing warmth and the promise of spring.

"Who are you?" Jules demanded.

Her mouth opened and a cluster of the sickly red and blue light ribbons squirmed out. The tips reached and searched for him.

Jules stepped back. "In Her name, I command you to begone."

He concentrated, pushed his aura down his arm to focus on his frozen fingers. The light intensified and he felt warmth return.

At first his fingers wouldn't move, still locked in place. Then they popped apart. The frost on the glove fell in a glittering shower. The instant her robe fell from his fingers, her skin seemed to blacken and burn, then she vanished. The faces in the windows above were gone. He heard screams and words he couldn't quite pick up. Then the air seemed to draw back for a moment.

He staggered and bony metal fingers grabbed his upper arms and prevented him from falling. He sensed the shape in front of him but it was like the rest of the pod, hardly more than smoke in the dark.

"Are you okay?" MAR-A said. "You made contact?"

Jules managed a weary nod. His exposed nerves and tissues burned. He couldn't answer with his face in his hand. Lifting it seemed harder than it should. He got it back in place and the connectors automatically found their points. It seized him, clamping down hard, and there was that instant familiar pain as it reintegrated with his nervous system.

The pod snapped back into reality around him. MAR-A skeletal face peered down at him from beneath its hood.

"Thank you," Jules said. His throat felt dry and sore. A yawn forced his jaw open and popped his ears. "Ugh. That was, *unusual.*"

"Are you steady?"

"Yes, thank you."

MAR-A released his arms. Despite his assurance, Jules had an instant to wonder if his legs were going to hold him or not. They did. His arms ached where MAR-A had gripped him.

"What was unusual?"

Jules shivered, looking around the dimly lit common area. "Let's go back to the transit module. I'm freezing. And I'd rather talk about this somewhere else."

"Very well," MAR-A said. It moved back in the direction of the bar and reached out toward the bra.

"Don't," Jules said quickly. "Don't bring it."

"It's a clue," MAR-A said. "An analysis of any DNA–"

"Later. Right now, let's get back to the transit module. I'm not sure it's safe here right now." Jules was already moving, heading for the corridor back to the airlock.

MAR-A left the bra and followed him into the passage.

The whole encounter hadn't taken long but Jules felt how it had drained him with each step. That sort of intense contact with the other side, the use of his own energy to break the connection, it had physical consequences. A nap sounded *really* good, but there were things to do before then.

Whatever was going on here, it was related to the crystal necklace the spirit wore. The way the tendrils were intertwined with the spirit, it suggested a parasitic sort of relationship, but he had never heard of a spiritual parasite like this before. The rough shape of the upside down cross had looked natural, but it was a dark symbol in some belief systems.

It didn't take long to reach the airlock. MAR-A had already opened the inner airlock hatch so they were able to go directly inside. The hatch closed behind them. The transit module's airlock was visible through the small window.

Something *moved* past the window. A shadow of a person?

A series of loud clangs rang through the airlock, like someone knocking on the airlock hatch in front of them with a wrench.

Terror suddenly hit Jules like a punch in the gut. *They were all going to die.*

The feelings weren't his, he realized. It was coming from somewhere else.

"Transit module clamps disengaged," MAR-A said. "Attempting to reestablish lock."

Transit module. Through the window, Jules saw the transit module airlock hatch close. Then it moved away from the window. A gap widened between their airlock and the module's. And continued to widen.

"Unable to reestablish lock," MAR-A said. "The transit module has disengaged from the *Olympia.*"

Jules walked forward to the outer hatch window. The transit module was moving away from the *Olympia* at a good rate. The rotational inertia translating into a decent velocity as it shrank in size.

"Can we recover it?" Jules said.

"No," MAR-A said, turning and leaving the airlock.

Jules backed away from the window. The transit module was turning as it shrank away. Or, actually, the *Olympia's* rotation was moving them up and away. For an instant, the light from the distant star illuminated the upside down cross shape of the transit module and forcibly reminded him of the crystal cross necklace worn by the spirit. He shivered and turned away from the window to follow MAR-A back into the passage.

The airlock hatch closed behind him. His feed announced a call from Bri.

Jules answered, opening a virtual window and inviting MAR-A to share the view.

Bri was in her office. Tee stood beside her chair, holding onto the back. Both looked concerned.

"What happened?" Bri said. "We saw the transit module detach."

"The clamps released the module and wouldn't reengage," MAR-A said.

Tee glared. "What did you do?"

"It wasn't MAR-A," Jules said.

"Are you sure?" Tee countered. "What if spirits were using it as a vessel again?"

He shook his head. "That wasn't the case. But I do think there's an inhuman spirit at work here, that was behind the module's release."

"There is another transit module," MAR-A said. "On the other side of the *Olympia.*"

"Don't touch it," Tee said. "We don't have a way to replace them."

"Can you intercept the one that was released?" Jules said.

Tee shook her head. "Not right now. We don't have that kind of power. We'll have to calculate the module's new orbit and then plot an orbit to intercept. It could take months for our orbits to intersect again."

"That seems likely," MAR-A said, earning a glare from Tee.

Bri said, "You said an in-human spirit. What are we talking about? A demon?"

"I don't know," Jules said. He was accessing the ship feed and his personal feed. He found the moment when he faced the woman with the necklace. Almost nothing of the encounter was visible in the ship's feed, but there was a dark person-shaped shadow as if rendered in smoke. His feed was better, revealing more details of the woman's face and the gleaming necklace. The other details that he'd seen came from his other sight.

He shared the images to all three. "Ship's feed and my own. I saw this spirit more clearly with my other sight. The crystal looked as though it was infecting her somehow."

The images only showed bright lines of vapor arcing out and back to the shape. He described they had moved, like living worms or maggots burrowing into a corpse.

Tee moved her hand from the chair's back, to Bri's shoulder. Bri reached across and up to clasp her hand. "You think this is the inhuman spirit?"

"I don't know," Jules admitted. "She was naked except for a robe and the necklace. MAR-A found a bra behind the desk. There may have been some sort of ritual that took place here."

"Ritual?" Tee said.

MAR-A answered. "A practice designed to increase a connection to the spiritual ecosystem, to commune with spirits, or harness spiritual energies."

"We don't know what their purpose would have been," Jules said. "But if the previous crew was engaged in some sort of spiritualistic practice, it might explain what is happening."

"Could it be the reason they disappeared?" Bri said.

"Possibly," Jules said. "It depends on a lot of factors we just don't know yet."

MAR-A's head lowered as it focused its eye on him. The lights around the sides brightened. "Really? This ship is haunted. The crew vanished. It seems logical that the two are connected."

Both Bri and Tee nodded at that. Tee said, "I hate to say, the killbot has a point."

MAR-A faced the virtual screen. "I am not a killbot."

Tee rolled her eyes.

"Whatever is the case," Jules said, "it doesn't change what I have to do."

"We should all leave," MAR-A said. "Rather than risk lives. Especially the children."

Bri shook her head. "We can't give up the ship. We have too much at stake."

"Is it worth Mel's life? Sara's?" MAR-A said, voice grinding like stripped gears.

"MAR-A," Jules said. "That's enough."

The droid turned and walked away down the corridor. It could still access the meeting feed, of course.

Jules faced Bri and Tee again. "Without the transit module, if we don't use the other one, we'll be forced to go pod by pod in order to get back to you. If we take the long way around it'll give me more opportunities to figure out what is happening and to find evidence. Maybe figure out a way to stop it. Or we can take the shorter way, and be back with you sooner. I can still try to figure it out, but I might be missing something important."

They exchanged a glance, some sort of silent couples-only communication passed between them, and Tee said. "We're okay here. Take the longer route, if it can help solve this. Figure out whatever you need for an exorcism, a cleansing, whatever you call it, to make this ship safe again."

"Is it safe for you to do that?" Bri said.

Jules shook his head slowly, unwilling to lie for them. "If these spirits are as hostile as they appear, probably not safe. We've dealt with similar situations before."

A text message from MAR-A appeared in his view. "We have?"

He ignored it and continued. "We'll take the long route around through the pods. We'll stay in touch. Keep close to one another, don't get isolated."

"Be careful," Bri said. She glanced up at Tee, then looked back. "*Both* of you."

Tee nodded. "Yes. MAR-A, I apologize for my outburst earlier. It's not your fault. Mel insisted I tell you if we talked."

"Apology accepted," MAR-A said. "I have no wish to endanger anyone."

"I know," Tee said.

Bri smiled at her and patted her hand.

"We're going to get started," Jules said. "We'll head spinward. You should be able to follow our progress on the system feed. Call if you need to."

"Okay," Bri said. "Bye."

Tee waved. Jules lifted a hand. Beside him, MAR-A copied the gesture. Then Jules ended the transmission.

He looked at the droid. "How far is it?"

"The *Olympia* has a circumference of over a thousand meters through the connecting airlocks, although the corridors from one lock to the next circle around the outer section of the pod, meaning that we need to traverse half the circumference of each pod to reach the next airlock, it essentially doubles the distance even if we move as quickly as possible from one airlock to the next and don't investigate each pod."

"We can't go straight through?"

The lights around MAR-A's eyes *blinked*. "No."

"Then we'd better get moving," Jules said. "I want to search this pod more thoroughly before we leave. We need to see if we can find any other clues."

"Searching each pod will delay our progress," MAR-A said. "It will add many meters to our travel."

Jules shrugged. "If we don't get answers, then it is all wasted time anyway. But let's power up the systems, shall we? I don't want to be stumbling around in the dark the whole time."

"Activating systems," MAR-A said.

Lights in the corridor ceiling brightened, the light spreading from the edges into the center. The air moved in a faint breeze that brought a hint of warmth.

Before he forgot, Jules stripped off his gloves and stuffed them in the jacket pockets. The fingers on his right hand still felt frosty from the contact with the spirit. He flexed them. It didn't seem like there was any permanent damage.

He unzipped his workall enough to reach his pockets. He took out a packet of *bounce* and two vials of blessed water. One, the vial he used to dispel the entity using MAR-A as a vessel, still half-full. The other was full. He stuffed the *bounce* into one jacket pocket and the vials in the other. He wanted to have easy access to them.

Jules zipped up and faced the corridor back to the common area. "Let's go look for ghosts."

Chapter 26

T HE POD WAS DEFINITELY less spooky with the lights on full. After the encounter with the spirit–spirits, if he counted the faces in the windows–the light was comfort.

Jules knew it was a false comfort. The light didn't stop the spirits. It still made him feel better as he surveyed the common area with distaste.

The lights showed the mess the previous crew had left behind. It hadn't only been the boxes and other refuse in the corridor, this whole place was a mess.

"The bots were ordered to stay out," MAR-A said, standing next to him.

Jules looked up at it. "Ordered? Who ordered them?"

MAR-A lifted empty hands. "Unknown. That detail isn't in the system. But there is a prohibition in the bot operator command system."

"What about the other habitation pods? Do they have the same instructions?"

"Yes."

"Including the Makkar's pod?"

"No, that one is not included. Tee Makkar removed that command when she came aboard."

Though he didn't want to encounter the spirit with the crystal cross again right now, Jules reached out with his other sight and started to walk through the space. Clothes were strewn about, draped on the furniture and discarded on the floor. The air had a stale smell to it, a result of the gradually warming environment.

The coffee table held the desiccated remains of food in open containers. A dried crusty area of carpet looked like someone had been sick on it.

There was more than simply a mess. He noted several sleeping bags scattered around the room, and pillows. Like the clothes, they were left discarded around the room.

"A sleepover party," he said.

MAR-A had shadowed him as he moved around the room. "What?"

Jules gestured at the mess. "It looks like a sleepover party. There were a lot of people packed into this space. That must explain the boxes in the corridor, they needed to get them out of the way."

MAR-A cocked its head, looking up at the windows on the cabin level. Jules followed his gaze, shivering as he remembered the faces there, but now there was nothing visible. His other sight was giving him vague impressions of people sitting, lying down, entwined together in sleeping bags. It was only the briefest flashes. Not spirits, only echoes of what had gone on.

"Why not use the cabins?" MAR-A said.

"I don't know. We need to take a look." Jules headed over to the hatch–closed–that led to the ramp leading up to the cabins.

MAR-A walked past him at the last moment and opened the hatch. Its body was between him and the hatch, so he couldn't get a good look when it opened. MAR-A didn't comment, just stepped through and started up.

Jules followed. He didn't say anything about MAR-A's protective behavior, but he appreciated the sentiment. Practically, MAR-A couldn't do much about spirits. It was still a nice protective gesture.

The corridor on the cabin level showed the same disarray. Refuse and boxes stacked against the wall beneath the hexagonal windows.

Suddenly Jules didn't want to open the cabins. The feeling came out of nowhere, but part of him recoiled at the thought of what they might find inside.

Except they had to look. MAR-A stepped over to the first cabin and the door slid open to admit them. MAR-A stepped inside, Jules followed.

The air inside the cabin was worse. It smelled of rot and blood. It was no wonder. A blood stain coated the center of the cabin's bed. It was mostly pooled in the center of the bed, though it had been smeared around.

"That's not good," Jules said.

"A person died on that bed," MAR-A said.

"I figured." Jules moved around the room. More blood was splashed on the walls and floor. It showed the savagery in the attack.

Smears showed where the body was dragged from the bed and dropped on the floor. Now that he was looking at it, the signs stood out.

It took him a second to realize that there was a figure standing in the door to the bathroom.

"MAR-A?" He gestured at the doorway, still without looking at it too directly. "What do you see there?"

"A doorway. I will investigate the bathroom. It may have been used for the disposal of the body."

MAR-A moved quickly across the room.

"Wait."

MAR-A stopped, head turning back to look at him with glittering eyes. "Why?"

Jules edged to the side. "I *see* someone there."

MAR-A swung back around, looking, and apparently not seeing anyone.

"*Look what they did,*" said the woman in the doorway. Her voice only a soft breath of air.

He didn't want to look. It wasn't something that he needed in his mind, but there wasn't much of a choice. He had to see.

He turned and *looked* directly at her with his other sight.

She was naked. Blood liberally coated her skin, which was pale beneath the gore. Slits showed in her flesh where she had been stabbed so many times that he couldn't judge the number. *Dozens of times.* Each was like a bruised, lipless mouth, carved into her chest, abdomen, arms and legs. She didn't turn, didn't move, but he *knew* that the wounds continued onto her back.

"*Look what they did,*" she repeated in that same deathly whisper.

He saw. He said to MAR-A, "There's a ghost. A young woman with dozens of stab wounds."

"That is consistent with the scene," MAR-A said.

It was, but that wasn't the point. Jules took a step closer to the woman. "Who did this? Why?"

She screamed, "Look what they did!"

She rushed at him, fingers reaching like claws.

Jules fell backwards in his attempt to escape. MAR-A moved instantly and caught him before he could hit the ground.

She was gone.

He regained his balance. MAR-A studied him. "What did you see?"

"The woman, the victim," Jules gestured at the bloody room. "She–"

The blood was gone. No spatters, no tracks, and the bed was bare and unstained. "It's all gone."

"I have a record of the scene," MAR-A said.

A feed window appeared on Jules's left. It showed the room they were in, the blood on the bed and splattered across the wall.

"It's gone now," Jules said. "She rushed me and then vanished as you caught me."

"The blood vanished at the same time," MAR-A said.

"It must have been cleaned up after the crime," Jules said. "It left an impression."

He cast a last look around the room. Nothing was out of place. It was a clean and empty cabin again, showing no signs of occupancy.

He thought of something, and said, "Check the repair bot logs for assignments to this cabin. See if they were directed here to clean it."

He wasn't sure if it mattered or not. But a log entry might tell them *when* the crime was committed, assuming it existed.

"I've initiated the search," MAR-A said.

Jules walked to the door with the combat droid following. Before he stepped out, MAR-A said, "There is no record."

Not surprising. He stepped out into the mess in the corridor, seeing the sleeping bags along the corridor. "Why sleep out here, if there was a cabin available?"

"No one wanted to go inside?"

"Maybe," he said. "Maybe squimish about sleeping where someone was murdered."

"It might explain the reason," MAR-A said.

It might. Or maybe it happened later, after whatever caused people to be sleeping out in the corridor.

The next cabin they opened showed plenty of signs of occupants. Like the corridor outside, there were sleeping bags, blankets, pillows, and other items to suggest that several people had been staying in this single cabin. Jules picked his way through the space, noticing that the warming air carried with it the smells of the people that had been here. A human scent of sweat, body odor, and sex. It was faint, but the odor sensors in his prosthetic face did a good job of picking out and identifying the traces.

MAR-A kicked through a pile of blankets. "Nothing useful remains."

"Useful for us," Jules said. He wasn't finding anything that explained what was going on here. "Scared people don't huddle together like this, if there isn't a reason."

"Unless a spirit tells us, we may not learn the reason," MAR-A said.

"Maybe. Can you tell? Are the other habitation pods like this one?"

"No," MAR-A said. "There are abandoned personal items like those we saw on the transit module. No indication that people had crowded into the space. An optimal crew complement would be eighty individuals. From what we've seen, it suggests that everyone on board came *here*."

He tended to agree. If something drove them all together into the same pod, then something must have happened. *Where did they all go?* The absence of anything concrete disturbed him. Had the crew left the ship? Willingly, or otherwise? Or where they still here, hidden away inside one of the pods.

"Come on," Jules said. "We need to clear this pod and then move on."

MAR-A moved on. Jules felt something watching them. He looked around and didn't see anything. The feeling didn't dissipate. It was like being watched by a crowd—only the crowd wasn't visible. He thought about the faces he'd seen up here, at the windows, watching them. The watchers were visible then as he faced the ghost woman with the crystal cross. But now, even unseen, he felt their presence around him as if they were just out of sight.

MAR-A opened each cabin door as they reached it. The rest were like the second cabin—crowded with personal items suggesting that more people had been staying here than it was designed to hold. But nothing more than that. They completed the circuit and MAR-A turned to face him. "I have access to the feeds. I don't see any need to continue this search."

Jules gestured and MAR-A sent him the feed links. He opened them as a single tall virtual screen, stacking the camera feeds for each level. Basement, sub-basement, and attic looked undisturbed. The people here could have spread out more by using those levels, but nothing in the cameras suggested they had.

"Okay," he said. "Let's move on to the next pod. What is it?"

"The Primary Medical pod," MAR-A said.

Jules accessed the feed again and displayed the camera views on the virtual screen. It looked quiet, no movement, but also no obvious signs of trouble. He dismissed the screen, knowing that MAR-A was monitoring it all anyway.

If there was anything Jules was going to see or stir up over there, it would likely be with his other sight.

"Okay," Jules said. "Let's go take a look. Maybe that's where they took our victim."

"Not all of the cameras are functional," MAR-A said.

Of course not. Jules resisted the urge to scratch at his face. The relief bought by the *bounce* was beginning to fade. He'd take more before they left the medical pod.

Chapter 27

THE SMELL GOT TO Jules the instant the airlock hatch opened to let them into the medical pod. It was the same thing that he had smelled when the doctors started testing his prosthetic face. Medicinal, sterile, and astringent odors that still didn't quite hide the ammonia and fear that hung in the air.

Sharp pains burned along Jules's nerves as he stopped a few steps out into the corridor.

"Are you scared?" MAR-A said.

Jules shook his head and forced himself to breath evenly. "No."

"You looked scared," MAR-A said. "Or ill."

"Closer to the the later," Jules said. It wasn't really a conversation that he felt like having right now. But he said, "The smell reminded me of being in the hospital."

"I understand," MAR-A said.

Jules looked up at the former combat droid. *Did MAR-A understand? How could it, never having lived?*

"The sense of smell is known to associate strongly with memories, especially traumatic memories," MAR-A said. "It is an effective technique to use in conditioning."

That wasn't the sort of understanding Jules had thought MAR-A meant. It made a lot more sense.

Jules accessed the feed, putting aside thoughts of what MAR-A might have done in the past, and opened a virtual screen to show the medical pod cameras. It was minimal coverage. Entrances, each airlock was monitored, and several common areas on the four public levels of the pod. Except for those core areas, though, there weren't cameras.

Patient privacy probably had something to do with that. Jules accessed the system map and studied it. The public levels matched those in the habitation pods, starting with the basement, the "main" floor, second floor, and a third floor above that. That all seemed based on the basic pod structure. There wasn't a wide common area rising between the levels, though. Each level was complete. The elevators were in the same position, but each level was divided up into different sections, offices, operating rooms, and patient rooms. A morgue occupied a portion of the basement level along with storage and several lab spaces. The design looked like a compact and efficient hospital packed into this pod.

He couldn't wait to leave. Except a hospital generally had records, and he didn't think the medical pod would be different. *If they weren't missing.* That was something they had to find out.

After he tackled the morgue. He wanted to check if the murder victim had been taken there. Or any other victims.

There had been alot of people packed into that habitation pod.

"I want to check the morgue first," he said. Following the schematic, he turned and went to the hatch on his left. The sign on it said, "No admittance."

When you had a former combat droid in the feed, such things didn't mean much. The hatch opened as they got close.

The corridor continued on between offices or examination rooms. Most of the doors were left open. He saw examination beds, medical equipment, all of it intact and waiting. The Makkars were brave to come out to a big ship like this alone–but the medical facilities looked good. It also begged the question of why people were packed into the habitation pod when they could have easily spread out into the other pods, including this one.

The woman with the crystal cross had to be part of the reason.

They reached the lift and the doors opened at MAR-A's signal. As soon as they were inside, it started down.

Jules opened a virtual screen with the feed from the Makkar's habitation pod. It looked quiet. All four were in the common area. Sara was playing some sort of game involving holographic characters with Mel. Bri sat in a chair on one side of the large room working on a tablet. Tee seemed to be pacing the room.

The lift reached the basement and the door opened. MAR-A went out first, black robes swirling softly around the droid. It moved silently into the space.

"Clear," MAR-A said.

This space looked both brighter and less welcoming than the floor above. The colors didn't help. It'd been done in a light blue, almost like ice. The cold air reinforced that idea. The space outside the lift was a sort of cubicle that opened into a larger reception area. There were notices on the walls, and a sign above the service desk that read simply, "MORGUE."

Jules walked around MAR-A into the reception area. A few chairs sat against the wall. Two sets of double doors led deeper into the floor, one on each side of reception desk. Part of him expected to see someone return to the service desk and was preparing to wait. The ordinariness of it after the last pod was disturbing. Those people had gone to that habitation pod and stayed there. *Why?*

"You should wait here," MAR-A said. "I will investigate and report."

"What? No. I need to see. Especially if there are other spirts here."

"I thought you might be scared. People are around death. Around me."

"I'm not," Jules said firmly. He looked up at the droid. "I'm not scared of you. Neither was Mel."

Lights glittered around MAR-A's eyes in a slow pulse. Then it said, "Which way do you want to go?"

Jules went right. Bolts of pain shot through his facial nerves. He reached into his pocket and fingered the packet of *bounce*. There'd be water here. Medications, but pain-relievers were less effective. *Bounce* relaxed the nervous system without a narcotic effect.

MAR-A slipped past Jules to push through the double doors first. Probably it was uneasy about the sparse camera coverage in this area.

It was being protective, even though Jules figured there was little call for it. Until MAR-A had activated these pods, they'd been at minimal life support. And there wasn't a lot that MAR-A could do about hostile spirits.

Besides the reception area, a couple offices were on each side of the short corridor before it opened into the wider space of the morgue.

A half-dozen advanced autopsy tables were set up in the room with plenty of space around each. Each was made of gleaming metal hexagons that Jules recognized. He'd seen other systems use these to create adjustable furniture. It was a sort of tile system. The hexagons could fold, contract, or expand as needed. Right now all of the tables looked the same, probably a standard human size, but they were most likely designed to accommodate different species requirements.

"MAR-A?" Jules walked closer to the autopsy tables. "Have you seen any evidence of alien crew?"

"The personal items we've seen are consistent with a human crew," MAR-A said.

Jules ran his fingers along the first table. He expected the hexagon tiles to feel textured, but his fingers couldn't detect any variation in the surface. It seemed like there was a clear layer over the top. It felt hard and cool to the touch, but evidently could change size with the tile.

He dropped his hand and studied the rest of the room. MAR-A was walking slowly around the room, looking at everything, each step making soft popping sounds.

Compared to other morgues he'd seen, this one looked advanced and essentially unused. Armatures with lights and other equipment hung from the ceiling above each table. The room also contained several workstations along the wall where they'd come in. Another opening on the other side of the room must be a matching corridor. Additional doors led off each side of the room into what must be laboratory and supply spaces. A wide sink where the coroner must scrub before performing an autopsy. The far wall, though, caught his attention.

It was refrigerated storage cabinets. Gleaming stainless steel with square doors arranged in columns and rows. Space for eighteen bodies, the form probably hadn't changed in centuries.

If the murder victim had been brought here, was it possible that her body remained?

Chapter 28

J ULES STOOD IN FRONT of the storage cabinets. Eighteen in total, the surface of the wall and the doors was gleaming steel. MAR-A finished its inspection of the room and crossed to join him.

MAR-A gestured at the doors. "Are you looking inside?"

"Yes." Jules inhaled deeply and let the breath out. His other sight wasn't picking up anything in the area.

He opened the door in front of him, swinging it out. An empty tray lay inside the rectangular space. He shut the door and glanced at MAR-A.

With a nod, he indicated the doors on that side of the space. "You check those. I'll look at the rest."

"Okay." MAR-A reached out for the door next to the one that Jules had opened.

He didn't wait to see what MAR-A found. He pulled the heavy handle on the next door down. The tray inside was empty.

So was the next beneath that. Jules moved over to the next set. He was reaching for the handle when MAR-A spoke with a voice like a saw blade.

"Here. This is the murdered woman."

Jules smelled a hint of decay and meat. He lowered his hand and turned to see.

The woman's ghost stood on the other side of the tray, looking down at her body. MAR-A stood at the body's feet, having pulled the tray from the locker.

She looked as she had in the cabin. Naked flesh covered in wounds. She wasn't quite substantial. That side of the morgue was visible through her and the image shook. Her head started to raise and Jules didn't want to look into her dead eyes. He dropped his gaze to the sheet-covered body on the tray. The sheet was thrown back to reveal her right leg. The flesh had the solidity that her spirit lacked. The pale tissue split where she had been stabbed in her leg. It all looked very pale, almost translucent and waxy. Probably because she had bled out on the bed.

And the salvagers' incomplete inspection meant that they hadn't found her body.

"*Look what they did,*" the ghost whispered.

"Do you want to see more?" MAR-A said, a hand poised to remove the sheet the rest of the way.

No. Except he needed to see. He nodded and walked closer, seeing the ghost standing on the other side of the tray. He felt the weight of her dark eyes on him. The odor of putrefaction was stronger now.

MAR-A pulled the sheet from the body. Jules winced. Cleaned of the blood, the wounds were even more garish.

They covered the body, crossing each other, until there was almost no area unmarked. Other cuts ran across her sternum, the 'Y' shape had to be from an autopsy. Those cuts were glued shut. Not the others.

"Look what they did," her spirit insisted, her voice rising with anger and frustration.

Look. Jules studied the marks and realized there was a pattern. He shivered as it snapped into focus. The stab wounds were so numerous that they had looked random, frenzied. But where the wounds intersected, they formed crosses. *Upside down crosses.* Like the crystal cross the other spirit had worn.

Still avoiding the ghost's gaze, Jules looked at MAR-A standing like death at her feet. He pointed to the wounds. "Do you see the crosses? Each of the intersecting wounds forms an upside down cross."

MAR-A made a growling noise. "Correct. Analysis shows an unlikely probability that this was random. What does it mean?"

"I'm not sure," Jules said, shaking his head.

"Look what they did!" The ghost was beside him, screaming the words this time.

He staggered back, raising his hand in an automatic warding gesture. He reached into his pocket with his other hand for the vial of blessed water.

His ears popped and she was gone, leaving her body as mute witness.

MAR-A's eyes glittered as it studied the space where Jules had been. "You saw something?"

Jules breathed to calm his beating heart and lowered his arm as he straightened. "Yeah. She–her ghost–was here. She kept saying, 'look what they did,' the last time very loudly. It startled me."

"Does startled mean scared?" MAR-A said.

"Not exactly." He moved back to stand next to the body. She'd been relatively young when she died. Older than Sara, but not by so many years. That disturbed him.

"Why her?"

MAR-A sounded like a tea kettle boiling as it answered, "What do you mean?"

"That habitation pod was full of people. We didn't see any other signs of violence. So why was she targeted?"

MAR-A said, "Humans kill. It is what your kind do."

This was old territory, and not something that Jules wanted to reexamine right now. "Granted. The method used looks ritualistic. She's young, barely of adult age, possibly younger."

"Virgin sacrifice." MAR-A said it in a smooth, passionless voice, made that much worse by the lack of sound effects.

"Possibly," Jules said. "We need to find her records. It might tell us something. Autopsy reports, examination notes, anything that explains what happened."

The hint of putrefaction in the air was faint. Her body was well-preserved. His breath caught. He'd seen her ghost at the crime scene, the scene itself. It had felt immediate, as if it just happened. But this had to have happened some time ago, before the ship was abandoned or whatever happened to the crew. She was killed, brought here, and *autopsied*.

"MAR-A, we need those records."

"I have not recovered any files of that sort," MAR-A said. "Recovery attempts are ongoing."

Jules looked back down at the girl's body. He gestured to MAR-A. "Cover her back up at least. Can you tell how long she's been stored here? Enough to give us a rough estimate of how long ago this happened?"

"It may be possible," MAR-A said. "The body has remained frozen. A core sample could help reveal an fluctuations in the decay rate, indicating variations in temperature. Even with systems on standbye, changes in heat dissipation from rotation and orbital proximity—"

Jules raised a hand. "Do it. Take the samples and analyze them. I'd like to know how long ago these events happened, even if we don't have the records."

"Is it relevant?" MAR-A said. "This procedure will delay our progress through the ship."

The pain beneath his prosthetic face felt like he had fire ants burrowing into his skull. He breathed in and out, watching his breath, until the sensation ebbed slightly.

"I need a break," Jules said. "I'm going to get some water and find a room to rest in. Come get me when you have the results."

"Very well," MAR-A said.

Look what they did, The ghost of that poor girl had said. He had to find out. It might be the clue to understanding what was going on here.

He pushed open a door to one of the rooms near the morgue. It turned out to be a small break room. A couch, a half-circle table against one wall, a bunk inset into another wall, and a kitchenette on the third wall otherwise taken up with cupboards. All of it in pale colors with small items left behind showing the inhabitant's character.

Jules headed first to the kitchenette and *felt* other presences in the space. Not spirits, but echoes of their energy remained in the place. He found glasses in a cupboard and tried the faucet. Water flowed freely–presumably the pod in standby still made sure the plumbing didn't freeze.

After stirring the *bounce* into the water, he took a long drink. It quenched the pain burning along his nerves in a wave of calm like sinking into a warm bath.

He closed his eyes and breathed easier in relief. Unfortunately, that was the only packet of *bounce* he had brought, and they had a long way yet to go.

Jules leaned against the counter and sipped the water. Considering what they had learned already, it might make sense to go back the way they'd come and take the shorter route to the Makkar's habitation pod. *Except* that would mean missing the Command pod that had housed the primary operations. Though systems could be accessed from anywhere on the ship–as MAR-A had demonstrated– the Command pod brought all of those functions together in the same place. The Chief of Operations and staff worked from there. Whatever had happened on the ship, that would have been the place at the heart of it, directing the response. It might have answers, if they could get there.

The *bounce* coursed along his nerves and cleared his thoughts. They didn't *have* to take the long way around to get there. If he could convince Tee to risk the second transit module, they could board it here and take it to the Command pod.

He looked up at the dark shape in the doorway.

"I scared you," MAR-A said, voice rattling.

"Sure you did," Jules said agreeably. "You have the results?"

MAR-A stalked into the room, hissing like a steam-powered engine. It stopped just beyond arms reach and a feed notification appeared in Jules's view.

He tapped it, opening the virtual screen and dragging it up to study as he sipped his *bounce*.

The results from the analysis of the core sample from the girl showed decay slowed by near freezing temperatures. She had died five years earlier, based on the preliminary data.

"Five years," Jules said. "Well-preserved for that long."

"The morgue cabinets are designed for preservation," MAR-A said.

Additional details in the report confirmed that the girl there was no evidence of postmortem violations. All the damage was done when she was alive.

Jules blinked and dismissed the report. He couldn't easily scrub the knowledge away. He looked at MAR-A's dark glittering eyes. Questioning the analysis would be a waste of time and MAR-A couldn't really understand the horror of what its analysis had revealed. He took a longer drink of the *bounce* to restore some calm instead.

"What are the chances that the Command pod might contain additional details about what happened on the ship?"

"Good," MAR-A said. "The emergency record logs should be intact. Do you have questions about my analysis?"

Jules quickly shook his head. "I'm sure it is thorough and complete. The emergency record logs can't be accessed remotely?"

MAR-A's head swung back and forth with a sound like a badly oiled hinge. "No. The ERL is proof against tampering and most anything that would destroy the ship. It is read-only and requires physical contact."

"And you didn't think to mention this before?"

"No."

Jules bit his lip. "Why not?"

"The Command pod was included in our plan. I would access the ERL when we arrived."

He made himself let it go. "Tee didn't say anything about it?"

"No."

Fine. "I'm going to call her, report what we've discovered and find out if she ever attempted to access the ERL."

Chapter 29

C ALLING TO ASK ABOUT the Emergency Record Log wasn't as easy as it sounded. Jules wasn't sure how to share what they'd already discovered about the *Olympia*. The murder victim might be the only member of the previous crew on board. *Or not.* He couldn't shake the feeling that the ship had more grisly surprises in store.

And making the call from the morgue was too creepy. Even here, in the break area. Jules took his *bounce* and led the way back up to the main floor to the reception area in front of the elevator. He sipped the water and opened the connection.

Tee appeared on his virtual screen. He recognized the close quarters of the sub-basement. She was alone as far as he could tell, sweat making her skin shine. She'd changed to a tank top that clung to her skin. It showed her thin, but muscled arms and shoulders.

"What?"

The way she looked, and the fact that she was in the sub-basement gave made him pause. "What's wrong?"

Tee ran a dirty hand through her spiky hair. "The same thing I've been fighting with since we got here. Readouts show everything as fine, but then it's freezing in some of the rooms. I fix something, then it breaks again. Repair bots have some sort of bug I haven't tracked down that causes them to forget their assignment and they wander off. Sometimes it's easier to identify what *is working* than what's broken."

"That sounds difficult to manage," Jules said.

"Not as bad with Bri back," Tee said. "She's got her work, but she can keep an eye on the kids while she does it."

MAR-A made a sound like a gasping fish. Tee's gaze fixed on it. "What's wrong with you, killbot?"

"MAR-A doesn't kill people," Jules said, irritated at her use of the unflattering nickname. Yes, MAR-A had been a combat droid, but that's not what it was now.

Tee nodded. "Sorry, MAR-A. What have you figured out? Anything on that creepy ghost with the crystal thingy?"

That wasn't the question he wanted to answer right now. He said, "Did you ever access the emergency record log?"

"No," she said. "It requires a physical connection and the command pod is on the other side of the ship. I've barely been able to manage the few pods we have running. Why?"

The lights flickered around Tee. She looked around with a groan. "Are you serious?"

"What's that?" MAR-A pointed at the shared virtual screen, at the narrow corridor behind Tee.

Jules didn't see anything.

Tee looked over her shoulder. "What?" She looked back at them, then back at the corridor. "Did you see something?"

"I detected movement," MAR-A said. "Is someone else there with you?"

She shook her head quickly. "That's not funny, k– MAR-A."

"No," MAR-A said.

The lights flickered again but stayed dark a fraction of a second longer. As the light returned, Jules caught of glimpse of what might have been a silhouette behind Tee in the corridor. But it was gone when the light steadied.

"It was there," MAR-A said.

"I saw it too," Jules said. "You should get out of there, Tee."

Tee was looking, turned away from the camera so he was seeing the back of her head. "I don't see anything."

"It isn't there now," MAR-A said. A second window appeared within the first as MAR-A added it to the call.

The new image showed a close up of the corridor as the far lights came on, but those closer hadn't yet. A silhouette of a person stood at an odd angle, as if pressed to the side of the corridor.

"There," MAR-A said.

"Oh shit," Tee said. "Okay, I'm going. If it gets cold in some of the rooms, so what. We're all staying together anyway now."

"We'll stay on," Jules said. "Just get out of there."

Tee moved to the edge of the space facing the corridor. She held a light now and pointed it down the space between the pipes and bundles of wires that ran between the equipment. The lights overhead flickered.

"What can you see on the cameras? Am I clear?"

"Go now," MAR-A said. "Listen to my voice. I will guide you."

"Hell," Tee said. "You'd better."

She ran forward into the space. Jules remembered how it felt down there, how closed in everything was. He set the feed to track her, switching cameras automatically as she progressed. She neared the area where they'd seen the shape and the lights flickered again. She put on burst of speed and the camera view on his screen switched to a camera ahead of her, looking toward her.

The lights went out behind her with a loud electrical snapping noise.

"Don't look back," MAR-A said. "Turn left at the junction."

Jules adjusted the spectrum on the feed and a bluish shape appeared in the dark behind her. Long, distorted limbs moved oddly as whatever it was pursued Tee. He fought the urge to tell her to hurry.

"Left?" Tee gasped. "That's away from the lift!"

"Don't take the lift," MAR-A said.

Its voice took on a more human warmth. "You'll be okay. Just go left."

More lights went out behind her. She was close to the junction now. The camera view switched to the junction, showing her running toward it. To the left, in the direction of the lift, the lights were out. More of the bluish shapes waited there in the dark.

She slid into the junction and caught a pipe as she swung around to the left. "Ouch! Shit!"

She flapped her hand as she ran away from the junction.

"Are you okay?" he said.

"Burned my hand on the pipe," she said, breathing harder. "Where am I going?"

"Straight through the next junction," MAR-A said.

Lights snapped on automatically ahead of her. The camera view jumped, tracking her as she ran. The lights ahead flickered as those behind died out. The UV view showed the shapes, a half-dozen or more, racing along the corridor. Some were crawling along the pipes and wires on the walls and ceiling, and didn't have any trouble keeping up with those running on two legs down the corridor. The way they moved was inhuman.

Lights that had just come on in the junction ahead flickered and died. Jules saw shapes closing in from each direction.

He couldn't help himself. "Run!"

"Yes," MAR-A said. "Faster!"

"Ugh," Tee said and sprinted forward.

The intersection wasn't quite dark since the lights ahead still lit the space. It didn't look like it was stopping the spirits racing to reach ear. Dark limbs reached out of the darker corridors for her. He saw dark gray pebbled skin, taunt tendons, and long fingers with too many joints.

Tee saw them too. She screamed and flailed about her with the flashlight as she careened through the intersection.

She got past and kept going.

"Right at the next intersection," MAR-A said.

"That's a dead end," Tee said.

"There's a vent," MAR-A said. "On the left side, three meters along the passage."

"Vent?" Tee panted as she ran. All of the lights in the section went out.

Jules felt his heart beat once, twice, and the lights came back. On the virtual screen, he could see the shapes coming after her. The lights kept dying behind her.

Not by accident. He caught glimpses of those dark hands reaching out and tearing at the lights before they went out.

Tee reached the intersection and turned right. The lights in that section went out.

Chapter 30

T HE AIR VENT ABOVE Jules made a faint clicking sound as the metal expanded from the warm air. As faint as it was, it sounded loud in the empty medical pod. A place that shouldn't be abandoned, it looked like doctors and nurses might return at any second.

His attention was focused on the virtual screen that floated in front of him. MAR-A stood a couple steps away, glittering eyes seeing past the space there were in to the Makkar's habitation pod. To the sub-basement where Tee had just run into the darkened corridor where MAR-A had directed her.

The inhuman spirits after her were already there, ahead of her in the dark. She wouldn't be able to see them, not in time. The light she carried bounced across the walls.

"Dive forward," MAR-A said, in a voice that had become progressively deeper and warmer. A voice that demanded trust. "Now. The vent is on your right."

On Jules virtual screen, he could make out the spirits as dark, glowing blue forms in the shadows, slight visible in the ultraviolet spectrum. *Because they were colder than the air around them.*

Tee dove for the floor at MAR-A's instruction. She landed in front of the vent and it opened, presumably under MAR-A's direction.

She felt around and found the vent. Jules could barely make it out.

"Inside," MAR-A said. "Crawl. When it reaches a junction, climb up."

Tee didn't argue. She threw the light ahead of her and squirmed into the small opening. Her shoulders barely fit. It wasn't a large space. She pulled her feet in right as one of the spirits reached for her.

The vent closed behind her. The spirit didn't, as Jules expected, follow her into the vent.

The lights came back on and the corridor space was empty on Jules's screen. He didn't see any sign of whatever had chased her.

"Is it still after me?" Tee panted.

The ventilation shaft didn't have cameras. Jules couldn't see her, but she was still on the feed with them.

"Not right now," Jules said.

"Keep moving," MAR-A said. "Climb the ventilation shaft up to the the main level. You can get out there."

"Seriously?" Tee said. "That's your plan?"

"Yes," MAR-A said.

"Isn't there a shaft in the basement level?"

"I wouldn't recommend it," MAR-A said.

Jules switched his view to cameras on the basement level. Few lights were on, but the UV filters showed shapes crouched on crates, hanging from the cages, or moving along the aisles.

"MAR-A is right," Jules said.

"Hell."

Less than a minute later. "I've reached the intersection. Up, you said?"

"Yes."

"How the hell?" Grunts and banging noises followed. "Damn. I got rolled over so I can reach the shaft. I'm standing up. How am I supposed to climb this?"

"Wedge your back on one side, feet on the other," MAR-A said. "You can do it."

"You might be able to," Tee said.

"I couldn't fit," MAR-A said.

"Come on, Tee," Jules said. "You need to move."

"Fine. I think I–got it."

Her breath was ragged as she started climbing. Jules could hardly imagine what she was going through.

He switched his screen view to the habitation level. Bri and the girls were at the table in the dining area. It looked like Bri had them studying or something. He opened a private feed window.

"Bri," he said. "Tee is going to need your help."

He'd already accessed the details from MAR-A showing where Tee would reach the main level. It was in one of the outer corridors. He sent her the location.

"She's coming out there."

Bri smiled at the girls as she stood up and moved away from the table. She held a tablet that she used to see what he'd sent.

"That vent? Why?"

"There isn't time," Jules said. "You need to get to her now. Make sure the girls stay where they are."

In case the inhuman spirits were waiting for Tee also.

"Okay. I'm going," she said.

She turned to the girls. "I'm going to go give Mama Tee a hand. We'll be right back. You continue your work."

"Okay," Mel said, her tone cheerful.

Sara didn't look as convinced. Jules thought she picked up on Bri's worry, despite her attempts to hide it. She was a smart kid, though, and glanced at Mel before saying in a fake bright tone.

"Need some help?"

Bri shook her head. She bent and kissed the top of Sara's head. "No. Help your sister study, if you're done with your own work."

"Okay," Sara said.

A text popped up on Jules's feed from Sara. "What's going on?"

"Later," he sent back. "It's okay."

He didn't think that would convince her, but it was hopefully enough to keep her attention on Mel.

Bri walked quickly out of the common area and broke into a run when she reached the corridor, out of sight of the girls.

"How much longer?" Tee gasped.

"You're nearly at the vent," MAR-A said. "Keep climbing."

Tee growled, and from the sound, kept climbing.

Bri ran through the corridors, turning to run down the stretch where the vent came out. The light panels overhead and in the wall flickered.

Please. Jules prayed. *St. Butler, protect them.*

He split his virtual screen, putting one on his left, and the other on the right. He set the right-hand screen to show the girls still at the table. Sara was helping Mel–and glancing now and that at the open hatch that Bri had gone through.

The left-hand screen show Bri, switching through the corridor cameras. She reached the section with the vent and dropped to her knees.

"Tee?"

"Bri?"

"I'm here!"

The vent swung up and open as Tee's spiky hair appeared in the opening. She fumbled for a grip and Bri caught her hand.

"I'll help you."

The lights in the corridor flickered again. Tee looked as if she might argue, but she didn't. She clasped Bri's hands. Bri braced her feet on each side of the vent opening and leaned back as she pulled.

Kicking and wriggling, Tee squirmed out of the vent and fell face first onto Bri. Bri wrapped her arms around her and pulled her the rest of the way out.

The vent swung closed.

"You should get back to the main living area," MAR-A said.

Tee and Bri scrambled up together and quickly kissed. Bri looked over Tee, running her hands down Tee's arms. There were scrapes oozing on her elbows and shoulders.

"What happened?"

Tee looked around, took Bri's hand and started pulling her back down the corridor. "Where are the girls?"

"They're studying. At the dining table."

The lights down the corridor behind them went out.

"Run," Tee said.

Jules looked between his two screens. The girls were okay, still studying, Sara keeping an eye on the hatch.

The women ran through the corridor. Bri had picked up Tee's urgency and ran all out now, even pulling ahead of Tee. Who was probably tired after fleeing through the sub-basement and climbing that shaft.

Another set of lights went out down the corridor.

He'd given Bri a vial of blessed water before he left to go with MAR-A. He asked her, "Do you have the vial?"

"Yes," she said, between fast breaths.

"Okay," he said. "When you get to the hatch, wet your fingers with it and rub it all around the hatch opening."

"Please, blessed Saint, watch over them," Jules prayed silently.

They reached the hatch into the common area and Bri stopped. Tee stopped a few strides in, apparently realizing that Bri had stopped. Sara was on her feet.

Tee pointed at her. "Stay there!"

Mel got up and wrapped her arms around Sara.

Bri pulled out the vial, uncapped it, and wet her fingers she traced her fingers along the hatch frame, wetting them three more times before she finished.

The lights down the corridor from the hatch went out. Bri stepped back. Tee caught her shoulder and pulled her back more.

"Move back," Jules said.

"Yes," MAR-A said. "Stay away from the hatch."

The lights in the corridor directly outside the hatch went out.

The women backed away until they were nearly at the couch. Sara and Mel came over and joined them. Tee swept her arm back, keeping the girls behind them as they faced the hatch and the dark beyond.

Dark hands reached out of the shadows toward the hatch and the frame began to glow. It was like sunlight had somehow come out from behind a cloud to bathe the hatch in light. The hands jerked back out of view.

Seconds later the lights in the corridor flickered and came back to life. Jules leaned back against the counter and crossed his arms.

"Are you okay?" he said.

Tee and Bri pulled the girls into a hug. Tee looked over at the bar, where the nearest camera was on the wall.

"We're okay. Thank you, what was that?"

Jules shook his head. "I'm not sure. Inhuman spirits, but I've never seen anything like them."

"That's not reassuring," Tee said.

"Will they come back?" Bri said.

Tee said, "What's to stop them from coming through the other hatches?"

It was a good point. "In my room. There are more vials."

"We can't just stay in here until the pod breaks down," Tee said. "We have to stop this, whatever it is."

"Come and get us," Jules said. "Take the other transit module and come here. Bring my baggage bot. It has my exorcism kit. If we get to the command pod, we might be able to figure out what happened and how to stop it."

Bri said, "And if the other transit module fails?"

Tee shook her head. "We can't race these things through the whole ship. I barely got away with MAR-A's help."

"Mama Tee," Mel said. "Are we going to go see MAR-A?"

He watched Tee and Bri exchange a look, more of that silent communication. Tee nodded.

Bri looked at the camera. "Okay. We'll do it."

"We'll be with you each step," Jules said.

"We need to grab necessities," Tee said. "The baggage bot will help."

They moved off to gather what they needed. Jules consolidated his windows into a single screen and divided it to watch the areas of the habitat pod.

If they could get out safely into the transit module, and it didn't disengage like the other one, it wouldn't take them long to reach the medical pod. Then they could all go to the command pod where MAR-A could access the ERL and see what light it could shed on their situation.

Hopefully enough to give him some idea of what to do.

Chapter 31

J ULES FINISHED HIS GLASS of water and sat it aside on the counter in the medical pod's reception area. The last of his *bounce* until the Makkar's arrived with his supply. It'd have to do. An itch had started under his prosthetic's left cheek, and he rubbed at the spot. The artificial skin of his face was flexible and smooth, but didn't feel quite the same as real skin. Another way that it remained in the uncanny valley. He usually avoided touching his face. Rubbing the spot did nothing to help with the itch. Which he couldn't really scratch, anyway, the tissues beneath were too thin and too damaged. Scratching it would risk infection.

He dropped his hand and tried to focus on anything else that would distract him.

MAR-A wasn't much help. The combat droid had folded itself down to sit in one of the waiting area chairs. Its head was bowed, hidden beneath his cowl. The dark robes pooled around it like spilled ink in the pale medicinal gray-white of the waiting area. A display showing the banded rainbow hues of a gas giant hung on the wall above MAR-A. The clouds and the planet itself weren't static, he realized, but in motion. It was a slow, somewhat mesmerizing display.

His virtual screen floated next to his left hand, the view divided into a grid showing the Makkar family. He'd set the feed to track each of them, in case they separated. He'd muted the feed. Right now three of the cameras showed the same view of the common area where Tee was with Mel and Sara. The repair bot from the kitchen was helping to pack supplies on a utility cart. The fourth section showed Bri in one off the cabins, quickly packing clothes and other items into a bag.

Whatever the entities were that had pursued Tee, they had stopped after encountering the hatch sealed with blessed water.

The reconciliation gave understanding of some of the principles operating the spiritual plane and the intersection with the material world. Spiritual energy could imbue objects or materials. It could be intensified through intention and ritual. That was the case with the blessed water. A Butlerian priest had blessed the water. It was a common item sold by the Church to protect and strength people.

The energy in the blessed water had repelled the spirits pursuing them. At least for now. It wouldn't last. Not unless he could take more definitive action.

The spirits themselves worried him. Form wasn't fixed in the spiritual realm, yet the inhuman spirits he'd seen were unlike anything he recognized. These weren't the same as the woman with the crystal cross, the ghost of the murdered girl, or the spirit that spoke through Mel.

She was the one he worried about the most. Her ability to make a connection left her vulnerable until she learned to control it. Right now, she was with Sara and Tee, apparently bargaining for more space on the utility cart, her arms overfilled with several stuffed animals.

MAR-A still hadn't moved in its seat. He knew it was monitoring key systems, the ship feed, the Makkars, and the camera feed from around the ship. Since the decision to use the remaining transit module and attempt to reach the command pod, MAR-A must also be bringing systems online and preparing the way.

Bri finished and headed back down to the common area with the baggage bot—now filled to capacity—crawling along behind her.

"I am excited to start this journey with you," it said to Bri.

Jules sighed and wondered again who had thought it was a good idea to give bots personalities. They weren't any smarter than most insects—they didn't need personalities.

Tee had found room for Mel's stuffed animals, including the fael wormcat that she held close to her chest. Real wormcats fed on blood, paralyzing and draining their prey. But they did have the cutest cat-like faces–as long as they didn't open their mouths. It made the furry serpents popular figures in animations and toys. A wormcat drinking a blood substitute through a straw wasn't nearly as terrifying, even if it was highly unrealistic.

Bri reached the main floor and reunited with the others. They faced the baggage bot since its mobile cameras gave them an easy point of focus for communication.

"We're ready," Tee said. "Has the transit module arrived?"

MAR-A, obviously monitoring everything, said, "Yes. It has docked successfully with your pod at the backside lock."

"What about the ghosts?" Sara said. "Are they out there?"

"No activity is showing," MAR-A said. "The way looks clear."

"That could change," Jules said. "Keep a vial of blessed water in hand. If you see anything, splash them with it."

Bri lifted her hand, showing the bottle she held between her index finger and thumb. "Got it."

She passed another one to Tee.

Mel stuck out her hand. "Can I have one?"

Bri looked at the camera, her gaze asking the question.

"Yes," Jules said. "It's better if you each have one."

He didn't add *Especially Mel,* though she was the one most likely to be targeted given her ability. He didn't want to worry them too much.

Tee said, "Okay. We're going." She put her hands on the girls' shoulders. "I'm going first. Sara, I'm counting on you to watch Mel. Mel, I'm counting on you to watch Sara."

That earned grins from the girls.

"I'm serious," Tee said. "You watch out for each other. I Mama Bri or I tell you to go on, you do it. No argument. Understood?"

Both girls nodded solemnly. Jules clenched his fists, digging his fingernails into his hands until his joints ached. He forced them to relax.

"We're going out past the kitchen through the secondary hatch. At the junction we go right until the next intersection and then left and straight on to the backside airlock. The transit module will be waiting there for us."

Hopefully, Jules said to himself.

MAR-A interjected into the conversation, "The airlocks are open. I'm in control of the transit module systems. We won't have a repeat of what happened with the other one."

"That's good," Tee said. "Thanks you."

Bri put her hands on the utility cart handle. "Follow Mama Tee to the transit module. We'll get aboard, ride it around to the medical pod to pick up Jules and MAR-A, and then we'll all take it around to the command pod."

Tee looked at the baggage bot's camera. "Still looks clear?"

"Yes," MAR-A said. "You should go now."

"Okay," Tee said. "Let's do what the killbot said."

"It isn't a killbot," Mel insisted.

"Come on, Melly," Sara said.

The baggage bot stood aside as Tee led them to a door near the kitchen. He hadn't even noticed it, thinking it was a closet or something. When she opened it, it revealed a short corridor with a hatch at the end. The hatch slid open as they neared it. Tee lifted her hand holding the vial of blessed water, but nothing jumped out at them.

"Let's keep moving," Tee said.

Jules thought she might be telling herself as much as the others.

She picked up the pace. He moved a chair out into an open space between the workstations. He sat down and waved away the virtual screen. Then he accessed the feed from the baggage bot to see directly through his cameras, with the bot's mics sending him the sounds. He didn't override its autonomous function to control its movements. He was piggybacking on its feed.

The bot detected his presence, confirmed his authorization, and said, "Oh boy, a passenger. Would you like to drive?"

"No," he said.

"What about an inventory of my current contents?"

"No."

"Should I access the ship feed for information about our destination?"

"No," he said. "Continue with current assignment and stop talking."

A text pinged him from the bot. "No texting either!"

Stupid bot personality. It'd almost be better to take over, but he didn't want to focus on driving the thing. He wanted to be there with the family.

It looked as if he was with them. The bot's feed wasn't any different than what he got from his prosthetics. Except that he was shorter this way as he coasted along behind Bri. She was pushing the utility cart, wheels rolling easily on the smooth floor. The bot had positioned itself *directly* behind Bri. It gave him a good view of her muscles beneath the tights she wore, but it didn't let him see much of what was happening up front. Now and then he'd get a glimpse of the girls or Tee as they hurried along. Mostly, though, they stayed in line.

They hadn't gone far down the corridor when the light panels flickered. Mel gasped.

"It's okay," Sara said.

"Keep going, girls," Bri said. She glanced back and met his–no, the baggage bot's–eyes. She couldn't know he was virtually behind her.

"Did you guys see that?"

"Yes," Jules said.

"Yes," MAR-A said. "The power interruption is consistent with behavior we've seen before. You might want to increase your pace."

Jules saw from their reactions that they'd all heard MAR-A.

"Come on," Tee said. "Let's hurry."

The pace picked up. Nothing that challenged the baggage bot, it glided along behind Bri seemingly without effort. Jules saw the energy expenditure increase, but the bot was in no danger of running out of power. The system would regenerate automatically when it entered a storage cycle.

They were running down the corridor now at a slow jog. Sara held Mel's hand, while she kept the stuffed wormcat toy clutched in her other arm.

On a private feed to MAR-A, Jules said, "How does the transit module look?"

"It's still secure," MAR-A said. "Attempts by an unidentified user to close the airlocks have failed."

"Attempts? From where?"

"Indeterminate. A wireless intrusion without a traceable source."

Maybe because it came from ghosts? He didn't suggest it to MAR-A, knowing that the combat droid would deal with the attempts no matter their origin.

From his perspective through the baggage bot, he might as well have been riding in a cart or other vehicle behind the family. Except that he *felt* the chair unmoving beneath him. The bot's speed varied and it moved from one side to another, all in an attempt to stay precisely behind Bri. If his prosthetics had compensated for him, the view probably would have caused him to be motion sick.

They turned at the first junction and kept going. The lights flickered twice, but didn't go out. MAR-A kept cackling to itself nearby, apparently it enjoyed foiling the attempts by their attackers.

The corridors seemed to stretch on, though it couldn't be that much more to the next turn and the final push to the transit module.

Then cold hands slid down and gripped Jules's shoulders.

Chapter 32

J ULES SCREAMED AS COLD fingers dug painfully into his shoulders. One small part of his mind promised to dismantle MAR-A a piece at a time if it was pranking him again.

Except he knew better. Whatever this was, it wasn't MAR-A.

"Keep going," he said, gasping for air as the fingers dug in with bruising force.

Despite the grip, his view continued to smoothly follow Bri and her family. They reached the intersection, and he caught a glimpse of Tee, intense and sweating, making the turn, beckoning to them all to come on. For a brief instant, she looked him directly in the eyes. Her gaze flicked on without pause. She hadn't seen him, she'd seen the baggage bot. And then she was running on ahead.

Jules pulled back in the feed so his view collapsed into a virtual screen floating to his left.

The reception area was dark. The lights had gone out. With no visible light sources, his prosthetic switched to infrared, scattering out beams to give him a black and white night vision view of the medical area.

MAR-A wasn't on its chair, he saw that much as dark shapes crowded around him and blocked the view.

They reached for him with long oddly-jointed hands that ended in long nails. He twisted, trying to see what held him, and caught a glimpse of more lean limbs and long fingers. As solid as they seemed, the shapes refused to stay in focus. They shifted in and out of view of his prosthetic. His other sight helped stabilize his view, but their silhouettes jittered and blurred like smoke.

A foul, sulfurous smell choked him. These things were inhuman spirits. The same that had terrorized the family, stirring up more spiritual energy. He didn't know how, but he'd bet they'd been responsible for the disappearance of the former crew.

Jules thrashed, kicking at the floor as he attempted to pull free from the grip that held him. Each movement felt like daggers digging into his chest. His shoulder bones creaked beneath the pressure.

More freezing cold hands seized his ankles, his thighs, and his wrists. The cold from the contacts burned his skin even through fabric. They held him fast, despite the suggestions of insubstantiality as he *looked* at them.

His view through his prosthetics flickered and cut out. Pain burned along the nerves of his face in white-hot fury as they *pulled* at his prosthetic.

Half-blinded by the pain, Jules accessed his feed and triggered the release of his prosthetic. Vision, sound, and smell cut out in an instant as he felt the contacts release. The pain washed across his face and eased down to random bolts shooting along his nerves. He gasped through his lipless mouth and screamed.

Shapes flickered into view as his *other sight* opened and reasserted itself. It wasn't like seeing things so much as imagining what was around him. Something anyone could do, envisioning the space around them with their eyes closed but his *other sight* gave his vision more clarity and persistence.

And it was clearer than ever without the prosthetic face.

Jules lifted his head and *saw* the spirits around him. Withered, blackened things, with skinny limbs and long faces like crescents. Blue and red energies swarmed and wriggled through and around them, burrowing and moving constantly through bodies like charred wood.

The same thing he'd seen earlier, with the woman with the necklace.

It was there, in these blackened monstrosities. As he looked for it, he found it embedded deep in furrows of their blackened chests. It gleamed with a slick, oily light, like an eye split into the shape of an upside down cross. The purple heart at the center *watched* him with something like hunger.

"Accept us, as we accept you."

It came from all of them, the spirits holding him and more that crowded around him. A whisper he felt on his skin and heard in his thoughts.

"Accept us. Accept us. Accept us."

The whispers battered at him like the wings of moths. He struggled against those that held him, but their grips were unyielding.

"No," he rasped, struggling to make the words. "St. Butler preserves me and protects me. She wards me from evil," he said, scratching out the words.

He *saw* a shine spread over his body as he tapped into the spiritual energy of his faith. "St. Butler preserves and protects me. She guides me in darkness."

The hands holding him slipped and struggled to maintain their grip. He fought against them, attempting to pull free, but they pressed down against him. More reached past the others to add their hands to hold him. They gripped his throat, his head, thighs, groin, and his biceps. The pressed and clutched at him everywhere.

"Accept us. Accept us."

He thrashed in real fear and it was ineffectual. They held him even with St. Butler's light on him. The glow began to fade.

Jules forced himself to relax back into the chair. Force wouldn't win this. Only his faith and his abilities.

"St. Butler preserve and protect me. She guides me with her light. She teaches me to know fear, and in knowing fear, to release it back to the darkness."

The litany calmed his mind. His vision clarified as he stopped fighting. They held him despite the light, but the light grew and shone through their blackened fingers.

"St. Butler preserves and protects me," he breathed in reverence. *They couldn't touch him. Not really.*

The spirits in front of him parted and another appeared. It was the woman he'd seen earlier, but transformed and blighted. Her skin was cracked and dried like a parched lake bed. Beneath it was the blackened and furrowed tissue of the others. The necklace was nothing of the sort now. Like the others it had sunk into her chest between her flaccid breasts and it pulsed like a blood-filled leech. It wasn't as deep as the others. It was closer to the surface.

The abomination plaguing her wasn't the worst of it.

She held out her cupped hands to him. In that shallow basin lay another of the crystal crosses. It writhed against her hands, dried tissues flaking away from the charred tissues beneath. The two short arms of the cross pushed against her hands like stubby legs, while the longer body thrashed like a tail. The stubby, pointed end lifted, and he glimpsed a circular mouth and splinter-sharp bone white teeth. Threads of blue and red waved at the ends of the stubby arms and two thicker threads danced above the end of the tail.

It hurt to look at the perversion. The colors sickened him. *This* was the inhuman spirit, the thing at the heart of this. Of each of those that held him. They weren't inhuman spirits themselves, but the spiritual husks inhabited by these loathsome things.

"St. Butler preserves and protects me," he said, not sure who he was trying to convince.

The withered husk that had been the woman stepped into the circle around him, her legs moving between his.

St. Butler's light shone between the husks but the things inside must be protected by the blackened and desecrated shells of their hosts. They held him.

And the one holding the cross creature meant to put it on his chest.

Chapter 33

C OLD RADIATED FROM THE inhuman spirit cradled in the hands of a dead woman. The parasitic spirits had burrowed into those on this ship. Not only spirits, he realized. Physical *things* had attached themselves to the crew. He saw the activity around him on the spiritual pane, but the hands that held him had taken on substance, as if the creatures existed in both panes and could shift from one to the other.

"St. Butler protects and preserves me," he said, each word a struggle without his prosthetic face.

The glow he sensed around his body, St. Butler's light, made the spirits holding him struggle. The cross things burrowed deeper into the husks sheltering them, trying to move away from the light. The red and blue tendrils woven through the blackened and distorted limbs, sank into the fissures and folds.

"St. Butler, save these souls," he said. "Protect them and cast out the inhuman spirits holding them."

The light he sensed around his body began flowing upwards over the hands that held him.

They screamed and jerked away as if burned, but the light stretched and didn't release them.

The one holding the cross creature lunged forward, hissing, as it shoved the cross thing at his chest.

Jules knew he didn't want it to touch him. His hands were free. He lifted them, seeing them in his mind's eye clothed in a nimbus of light, and clasped the hands holding the cross.

The spirit screamed as the light moved up from his hands to envelop her fingers. Tendrils lashing, the cross thing leapt from her hands at him.

He had a sense of movement and a scarred metallic hand caught the leaping cross thing before it could touch him. Tendrils from its tail and stubby limbs lashed at the fingers holding it and didn't find purchase.

"St. Butler preserves and protects me," Jules said. He turned his blind eyes to look where he sensed the presence that held the creature. "Where have you been?"

MAR-A's voice grated like stone rubbing on stone. "Investigating the wounds on our murder victim. I discovered something interesting."

The spirits had faded back into the darkness, fleeing from the area. Except for the creature MAR-A held. It's sickly aura radiated cold, but it couldn't find anything about MAR-A to infect. And naked and alone as it was, it didn't seem to be able to escape into the other plane. It needed a host.

"The wounds were from something *removed* from the body," Jules said. He gestured at the thing MAR-A held. "Things like that."

"You saw something," MAR-A said, voice accusing.

"Yes," Jules said. "Their infected spirits. They've become the blackened husks we've seen as these things consume them. She must have had one of these things on her for each of those wounds."

"I need to secure this specimen," MAR-A said.

Jules nodded. "How are the Makkars?"

"Well. On their way in the transit module. They will arrive in thirteen minutes."

Jules felt behind him for the chair and settled back into it. He waved a hand to MAR-A. "Take that thing away. We can't afford it escaping."

"It won't," MAR-A said.

"Do you see my prosthetic?"

"Yes. It is near your left foot."

"Thank you." Jules bent down and reached out, almost sensing it, until his questing fingers found it.

MAR-A was moving off, looking for something the hold the cross creature.

By feel, Jules turned the prosthetic around to the proper orientation. He gritted his teeth and lifted it up to settle it into place.

Pain surged along his nerves as the connections clamped on. He gasped and drew in a breath, feeling it pass through his nose, and then the exhalation across his lips. His senses returned and brought with them the scent of fear sweat, the sounds of systems operating again, and bright lights that made him blink and squint for an instant before his eyes adjusted.

There wasn't any sign around him of the close call. He heard MAR-A in one of the adjoining rooms, the feed showing him it was a supplies closet. His virtual screen showed the view from inside the transit module from the cameras and the baggage bot's feed.

Jules pulled the window over and expanded it. He didn't go into the bot's viewpoint again. Right now, he preferred to keep an eye on his immediate surroundings.

Everyone was in the main area of the transit module. Bri and Tee sat beside each other at one of the control stations. The girls were sitting on one of the couches, facing each other, legs folded up beneath them. His quick impression was that this transit module had fewer personal items left on the stations. It looked less used, with fewer signs of wear.

But the important point was that they were okay. He accessed the feed and set up a private link to Bri and Tee.

"We had an incident," he said. "We're okay. And we learned something about what is happening."

"What happened?" Bri asked, her voice soft. On his virtual screen he saw her look over at the girls.

There were less than ten minutes until the transit module arrived at the medical pod. He kept the explanation brief, telling them that more of the spirits that had chased Tee had attacked him and had attempted to implant him with the cross creature.

"An alien?" Tee said. "That's responsible for the previous crew's disappearence? I thought you said that it was a crystal?"

"It appears crystalline, but it is a living organism."

MAR-A came back into the reception area carrying a clear jar, top sealed, with the thing inside it.

"We captured one," Jules told them. "We can show you when you get here."

Tee shook her head. On the screen he saw her face harden. "No."

MAR-A's head cocked to the side as if listening. Jules was sure that the droid was monitoring the conversation along with everything else.

"No?" Bri asked. "What do you mean?"

Tee turned to her. "They say they have this thing contained—but what if that's a lie? We can't risk it. We can't risk being exposed."

"Tee," Jules said. "I assure you it—"

"No, Jules. I'm sorry. We're not going to stop at the medical pod. We'll go on to the command pod. I'll access the ERL."

"We can't –"

Bri's protest cut off as the view on the virtual screen vanished. Jules tried the feed connection to the transit module and found it blocked.

Tee had cut them off. And she was leaving them here.

Chapter 34

J ULES ATTEMPTED TO REESTABLISH the feed connection to the transit module but it failed.

"MAR-A? Can you get them back?"

MAR-A's eyes flashed in a swirl of scarlet lights. In a voice like teeth grinding, it said, "No. Tee has disconnected the feed systems in the transit module. Ship telemetry shows the transit module accelerating."

Jules pressed his hands together and leaned forward. His beads clattered as if the spirits they contained were trying to speak to him. The things he needed to perform an exorcism were in that transit module, with the baggage bot. The ERL might hold the keys to explain these cross creatures. It should have a record of what happened. That could be crucial to the steps he needed to take.

"Can Tee cut us out of the feed connection to the command pod?"

"No," MAR-A said. "Those systems are too complex and I've control the access codes. I could shut them out of the *Olympia.*"

"I don't know that it would protect them," Jules said. "We need to get there."

"We can travel through the pods to the command pod," MAR-A said. "It will take time."

"More than we have, I think," Jules said. "I don't think that those things have given up."

In the container MAR-A held, the creature had used the longer blue and red ribbons of its tail to pull itself upside down again. Tendrils from the stubby arms pressed against the glass to hold it in position. Still like that, it again resembled a crystalline cross that shone in the light. It looked harder.

A defensive reaction? Maybe. It might go dormant when it lacked access to a host upon which to feed.

"There is one other option," MAR-A said, voice creaking. "You won't like it."

"What?"

MAR-A explained its idea and was right. Jules didn't like it. And it seemed like they only way.

MAR-A secured the cross parasite in a padded container. A strap held the container against MAR-A's back. When it was ready, they went back to the pod's lift.

"How much time do we have?" Jules asked, as they entered.

"We must hurry," MAR-A said. "The transit module will pass in minutes."

The lift closed and accelerated up through the pod levels fast enough to stagger Jules. MAR-A had obviously overridden its controls.

The doors snapped open and MAR-A was pushing him out, shoving him as it broken into a run. Jules ran faster and MAR-A relaxed the pressure.

They sprinted along a corridor that curved around past closed rooms. A shadow flitted across the corridor ahead.

"We're not alone," Jules gasped.

MAR-A didn't answer. It grabbed his arm and swung him around into an intersecting corridor that ran out toward the pod's outer shell.

Hatches opened. They entered a utilitarian corridor, passed another hatch, then a final room with an airlock on the far side. The inner hatch was already opening.

Jules fought back the panic growing in his mind. His face burned all over again. This brought back too many memories of the accident.

"St. Butler preserve and protect me," he breathed.

MAR-A pulled a plastic packet out of a locker beside the airlock. He shook it it and it unfolded to into a silvery bag. *A body bag.*

Literally. An emergency recovery bag. It was meant to quickly enclose a person with a suit leak so they could be brought inside.

Jules forced himself to move, stepping forward into the bag as MAR-A dropped it over him. The bag automatically sealed behind him and air hissed into it from attached containers. It smelled of metal and ozone. He held his breath and then exhaled slowly.

Until MAR-A's hard arm hit him across the middle and forced the air out in gush. He was as helpless as in infant in MAR-A's arm. He couldn't see anything in the dark of the bag. His other sight was too unfocused, to distracted with fear as he felt himself carried quickly into the airlock.

The airlock depressurized. He heard the air hiss away and the bag crackled as it expanded and stretched out stiffly around him. MAR-A's arm disappeared and Jules and the bag swung down. He tried bracing his hands against the sides of the bag and was terrified that his fingers would tear the thin material.

Sounds outside were gone with the air. He sensed the space opening around him and felt the vibration as the outer hatch opened.

MAR-A moved forward and stopped.

Jules pictured the airlock, small and high up on the pod. One of the maintenance locks. If the transit module had stopped, the tall central tower of the module would have mated with this lock.

Except it wasn't stopping. MAR-A planned to jump out of the lock carrying Jules in the bag, and catch a grip on the module.

The velocity was going to be incredible, but MAR-A was sure it could handle the forces. There hadn't been time to get Jules into a suit. The emergency bag was the only way for him, and MAR-A would have to keep a grip on the bag too, which mean catching the transit module one-handed.

"St. Butler preserve and protect us," Jules said.

Then the bag was swinging forward so fast he was pressed hard against the material. It forced the air from his lungs. A part of his mind expected the bag to tear like tissue paper and spill him into space. He had no idea what was happening.

What if MAR-A missed the jump? If it couldn't get a grip? At the speeds the ship rotated, they would shoot off into space like the other transit module.

A massive weight hit Jules's chest like a building had fallen on him. Then something hard slammed into his left side.

Blackness enveloped him.

Chapter 35

J ULES WOKE LYING ON a hard floor–which was better than drifting weightless through space until the air in the rescue bag ran out. Or he froze.

It didn't feel like much time had passed and a quick check of his overlays showed he was right. Only a couple minutes had passed. He was still in the rescue bag, the sides wrinkled now that it was back–apparently–in a pressurized environment. His arm and leg on his left side ached with a deep bruised feeling.

He heard the sound of a hatch closing from outside the bag. Then something seized the bag and dragged it and him across the floor.

"Hey! MAR-A? Let me out." He *hoped* it was MAR-A out there and not some alien infested spirit.

The dragging stopped. The bag rustled as someone messed with it and then the seal opened, peeling back away from his face.

MAR-A's dark head looked down at him, eyes glittering. "I scared you."

"Yes," Jules said, reaching up a hand. "I was terrified the whole time."

MAR-A clasped his hand and pulled him easily up to his feet. Jules stepped out of the bag, let go of MAR-A and kicked the bag away.

"Remind me to never do that again." He looked around. They were in a small chamber with two suit lockers on the right side of the room. It narrowed in front of them to what looked like a lift door. He pointed.

"That way?"

"Yes," MAR-A said.

The case was still strapped to MAR-A's back, so they hadn't lost their sample either. "The specimen is intact?"

MAR-A pulled the case around to its front, and opened it. The glass specimen container was unbroken. It didn't look like the crystal cross creature had shifted at all during their crossing. Its tendrils still held it in place.

"Okay." Jules gestured. "Close that and let's go see how the Makkars are doing."

MAR-A snapped the case closed and engaged the locks.

The lift door opened as they approached and Jules tensed. It was empty. His other sight didn't show anything either. He glanced at MAR-A but even its eyes didn't express anything. He didn't ask if it had opened the door.

Once inside, the lift descended quickly. From the other transit module, he knew that it would open directly into the main work area at the module's junction.

Tee *probably* didn't have a weapon. He couldn't be sure, though. He didn't doubt that she could rig something up.

He checked for feed access, trying to reconnect with the baggage bot. Maybe get a view into the room to see what was going on. They had to know the lift was coming down. He still couldn't find a connection.

They were nearly there. He motioned for MAR-A to step back, and stepped back himself to the side of the lift. It wasn't much cover, but it might protect them a bit if Tee opened fire with something. Like fire. Or other things that would make his day that much worse.

The lift stopped. The door slid open.

He heard a loud popping noise and two metal prongs trailing thin wires shot into the lift, hit the back wall, and fell to the floor. Which fortunately, wasn't conductive.

"Shit!" He heard Tee say.

MAR-A stepped into the doorway and swept up the wires with one twist of its hand. It yanked and there was another cry. The taser bounced across the floor and stopped when it hit MAR-A's foot. It cast the wires aside.

"We aren't here to hurt you," MAR-A said. "You don't need to be scared."

Jules looked out into the common area. Tee and Bri stood in front of the door, Bri holding a large wrench. Tee's hands were empty, but raised defensively in front of her. It took him a half-second to see the girls, peeking over the back of the couch.

He stepped into the open in front of MAR-A, moving slowly out of the lift. He didn't try to approach them. He held up his hands, palms out.

"It's okay. We got away." He used one hand to pull his shirt to the side and down, showing the top of his chest.

"I'm not infected. These things, they can't do anything to MAR-A. I need to see what is on the ERL so I can plan how to do an exorcism of these things. I can put an end to it, Tee, if you give me a chance."

Bri lowered the wrench then tossed it away onto the nearest workstation. It clattered against the wall.

"Bri!" Tee reached out, trying to catch Bri's arm.

Bri side-stepped and shook her head. "We have to trust them, Tee. What else are we going to do? If we want a chance at surviving this and keeping our ship, we need them."

Tee crossed her arms. "How can we know if they are influenced by these spirits?"

"We have to trust them," Bri said. "That's been the case all along. You know how long it'd take to get another transport out here to take us off. We don't have that kind of time."

Tee obviously wanted to believe Bri. She was just scared and trying to protect her family.

"The *Olympia* is like a sunken ship in the ocean back on Earth, forming an artifical reef. Only here, it's spiritual energy. Some of the spirits were already here, members of the previous crew that died. I think the one that spoke through Mel was like that."

Mel had risen up behind the couch. Sara stood up too, and then they both came out and carefully approached their parents. Bri reached out to them, and they gratefully went to her. She stood behind them, arms holding them both close.

"These other things infested the ship," Jules explained. "It seems like their hosts sustain and protect them—and give them the energy to move from one plane of existence to another. We need to stop them. Both from infesting any of us, but also to make sure they never come into contact with anyone else."

"Five minutes until arrival at the command pod," MAR-A said. "Decide."

"How did you get away?" Tee said.

Jules glanced at MAR-A. "Show them."

As MAR-A pulled the case around to open it, Jules said. "MAR-A captured this one before they could put it one me."

MAR-A opened the case cautiously. When it was clear that the creature hadn't escaped, MAR-A opened it fully and tilted it to show them.

Jules was relieved to see that the crystalline creature hadn't changed its position.

"It's pretty," Sara said, her voice soft.

"That's alive?" Mel said. She tried to take a step forward, but Bri held her back.

"You stay here, miss. It's dangerous."

Tee did take a step closer, eyes narrowing as she studied the creature. "It's still alive? It looks like a crystal cross."

"But it's upside down," Sara said.

"It's alive, as far as we can tell," Jules said. "I saw these infesting the spirits on this ship. Those tendrils that are holding it in place in the jar–those were intertwinned all through the spirits. The spirits looked burned, like charcoal, like these things had consumed their spiritual energy."

Tee looked up. "And they can move between planes of existence?"

He nodded. He gestured at the specimen. "Not on their own, apparently. I suspect that they need a spiritual host."

"So they took the bodies with them?"

He shrugged. "I don't know. The girl that was killed, she had dozens of cross-shaped wounds on her body. We think that she was infested with these things and the crew cut them out."

Bri scowled and held her girls tighter.

MAR-A snapped the case closed and secured the latches. "We're nearly there. What is your decision?"

Tee glanced at Bri, then back to them, and nodded. "We'll help. However we can. Sorry about trying to leave you back there."

"I understand," Jules said.

"I don't," MAR-A said, voice sizzling like boiling oil.

Jules left that one alone and crossed the room to where the baggage bot crouched out of the way.

"Hey there," Jules said. "I need a few things."

The bot stirred, lights animating. "What do you need?"

Jules asked it for packets of *bounce*–his face was in agony, painkillers for the bruises on his side, and his exorcism kit. Compartments opened and small arms extended, offering him the items requested.

He accepted them. Slipped the strap of his exorcism kit over his shoulder. "Thank you."

"My pleasure," the baggage bot said with artificial enthusiasm.

The transit module began slowing as the clamps engaged. Jules crossed the room to the small galley. Mel was asking MAR-A to see the pretty crystal thing, which caused both parents and Sara to say "No!" at the same time.

MAR-A's voice was gentle as it said, "It is dangerous."

Dangerous. True, and it still didn't quite encompass what the creature was. He'd never imagined something like it. A cold, inhuman, intelligence that spread like a disease.

He reached the galley. Water flowed easily from the faucet. He filled a glass, stirred in *bounce*, and then swallowed the pain-killers with a large swallow. As the *bounce* radiated out through the angry nerves in his face, he sighed with relief. He turned to face the family, leaning against the counter while he sipped his *bounce*.

Bri walked over to him. She reached out and touched his arm. "Are you okay?"

He shrugged and smiled. "Relatively." He lifted the glass. "This helps."

"What do we do if they come again?"

He touched his exorcism kit. "I should be able to handle that. Use the water, if you have to."

"Where do these things come from?"

He shook his head. "I don't know. I haven't seen something like this. Most intelligent life has a portion of themselves rooted in the spiritual plane. Even species with very different intelligences, like dogs. Our spirits shelter in our bodies. In a very real sense we inhabit both planes in life. These crosses infect the host, feeding with those tendrils on the spirit and body. They can move between both planes. But I don't know how or where they came from. Or how the crew on the *Olympia* came into contact with them."

The module came to a slow stop. They swayed. He pushed away from the counter and drained the last of the bounce.

"Let's go see if we can find out," he said.

Chapter 36

M AR-A LEFT THE TRANSIT module first, still carrying the secured case holding the cross creature in the sample jar. Jules followed it out into the command pod.

The light panels were on. The temperature wasn't warm–his breath fogged the air–but it was tolerable. It smelled of metal and old filters. Starting the systems must have blown out the cobwebs, so to speak.

It didn't look like the habitation pods, or the medical pod. The layout was different, the airlock opened into another chamber, round, with a high ceiling and four curved benches. All of it done with soft bluish carbon panels. The light panels were white, a large circle in the ceiling and two bands circling the walls above. Gaps between the benches gave access to the hatches leading out of the room, including the one that they had come through. The rest were all closed.

MAR-A stopped in the center of the room, head swinging, as if it couldn't decide which of the other three hatches to take.

Jules walked up beside it. The family was coming into the room behind him, quiet for once, with his baggage bot bringing up the rear.

"Is there something wrong?" he asked MAR-A.

MAR-A looked at him, then shook its head. "I anticipated the likelihood of an attack at 83 percent."

"Glad it didn't happen," Jules said. He touched his exorcism kit bag where it hung against his hip. *They wouldn't catch him as unprepared this time.*

"They may fear we will harm this." MAR-A placed a hand on the case it carried.

"Possible," Jules said, still studying the room. It appeared to be a sort of waiting area. "What's the purpose of this room?"

"Decon," Tee said, standing at his shoulder. She pointed at the walls. He saw faint lines he hadn't noticed before. "Those panels open into individual deconamination compartments. They can be adjusted to accommodate different species, different types of contaminates."

"Why? What could they be exposed to?"

"Volatiles on the comets," Tee said. "Some ices are toxic. Some comets have also been known to support phages, viruses, or even microorganisms."

Life was abundant in the universe, Jules knew. It was one of St. Butler's insights. The Principle of Life stated, *In all places where life may arise, it will arise within the span of the Universe. Life is the fundamental expression of the physical and spiritual faces of the Universe.*

It meant that life might arise on a comet, perhaps through the slow evolution as the comet orbited closer and farther away from its parent star—or in being captured by a neighboring star. He simply had not considered that possibility, usually thinking of planets and moons as the origin point of life. He should have known better.

Mel jumped up on one of the benches and walked along it, arms out to her sides. Sara crossed her arms and looked from Mel to Bri, as if to see if their mothers were paying attention. Bri clearly didn't notice as she took Tee's hand. "What do we do now?"

MAR-A crossed the chamber to the door directly across from the airlock. He pointed a bony metallic finger that uncurled with a clicking noise.

"This way," he intoned.

The hatch opened. The lights in the short corridor outside flickered to life.

Jules stepped up next to MAR-A. He took a vial out of his pocket and poised his thumb on the stopper.

"Let's go, then."

From behind them, he heard Bri his for the girls. MAR-A strode forward and Jules matched his pace. The family followed behind, trailed by the baggage bot. Jules kept his other hand on the exorcism kit.

The corridor was made of the same material as the decon room. The panels lit it with a bright bluish light. It was a short corridor before it opened into a wide and high space ahead.

Stepping out, Jules looked up and up, past levels of balconies. At the peak of the dome far above, a wide window had a clear view of the comet clutched at the center of the *Olympia.*

Now, even more than on their approach when they arrived, it looked like a baleful skull glaring down through the window at them. Particles drifted from the round pit where the harvester arm dug into the comet. It was like a dark and empty eye socket spraying out tears. The pitted and scarred surface of the comet didn't look that different than his actual face beneath the prosthetic face. A sharp sympathetic pain stabbed through his right eye as he watched the arm digging into the pit. Another arm cast an electrostatic net that guided the particles down into the hollow at its base, processing the liberated ice before routing it to the storage pods.

"Jules?" Bri touched his arm.

He started.

MAR-A loomed up over him, saying accusingly, "She scared you."

"Startled," Jules said.

MAR-A pulled its head back. Yellow lights circled its eyes as it considered this.

Jules looked at Bri, meeting her green eyes. "Was that comet already captured when you arrived?"

Bri nodded. "Yes. The harvester systems weren't active."

"I started it up while Bri went to get help," Tee said. "It's mostly automated. Why?"

He turned and looked back the way they'd come. At the decon chamber. *In all places Life may arise, it will arise within the span of the Universe.*

He looked back at the women, at MAR-A, and the girls watching, and opened his other sight wide.

Red and blue ghostly tendrils reached out of the case MAR-A carried. They waved around in gently seeking motions like something from the bottom of a sea. *Spirit eater.*

He looked again at the large space of the command pod. The center was clear. Stations surrounded the central area. More levels rose above, each open balconies that looked out into the central area. More stations on each level. All adjustable, designed for flexibility. It wasn't the stations that concerned him.

It was the spirits that crowded the pod. Their numbers filled the space around the central area, the balconies above, and the space behind the family. Blackened, withered, and drained, most of the spirits were original human—though twisted and warped now into malevolent demonic shapes. Here and there were other forms, a Cetarian turned into a near skeletal wraith, a Lasserite turned the color of white ash. Some others he couldn't identify, they were so transformed.

By the *spirit eaters*. The blue and red tendrils twisted and writhed through the drained husks of the spirits they fed upon. At the heart of each, burrowed in until barely visible, glinted the sickly upside down cross shapes of the *spirit eaters*.

"St. Butler preserve and protect us," Jules said. His thumb automatically unstopped the vial he held. With the other, he reached into his exorcism kit and his fingers found the worn smooth cover of his Butlerian Bible.

He pulled it out, lifting it.

"It's a trap," he said to the others. "They're here."

Chapter 37

G HOSTS INFESTED WITH THE *spirit eaters* crowded the balconies, the floor, and the passage behind Jules, MAR-A, and the Makkars. Then the ghosts began wailing.

It sounded like rage and fear. Jules lifted the Butlerian Bible he held higher. Ghostly blood-red and starved-blue tendrils reached out from the case MAR-A carried, the creature inside seeking a connection.

He wanted to tell MAR-A to throw it away before it could make contact with one of them. Instead, he partially covered the top of the vial with his finger and flung drops of the blessed water at the case.

The tendrils thrashed and withdrew back into the case. The gathered enslaved spirits screamed with rage.

He saw Mel clap her hands over her ears, her eyes huge and round as she looked at the approaching spirits.

The light panels in the command pod dimmed and flickered.

"Make a circle with the water," he said to the others. "Quickly!"

Tee didn't hesitate. She flicked off the stopper and started pouring a thin stream of water out on the deck as she moved around MAR-A and began the circle. When it ran empty, Bri passed her another, and Tee continued.

It was his other sight that held most of his attention. The spirits, or more accurately, the *spirit eaters*, saw the danger. They'd been stopped at the hatch from catching Tee before. They surged forward en masse, many of those on the balcony simply leaping out into the space.

Jules lifted the book, holding it high, as he said, "St. Butler preserve and protect us from all evil in our hearts or the hearts of others."

He swung his arm, casting a spray of droplets at the approaching infested spirits. In his other sight, the drops were like stars, bright specks that streaked out into the teeming mass of infested.

Each droplet, when it hit the infested, blazed brighter. Tendrils in the area touched retracted back toward the cross shape of the *spirit eater*.

"Help her," Mel said, handing a vial to her sister.

Sara nodded, took the vial and the one she already held, and went to the spot where Tee had begun the circle. She poured out water and quickly moved along the circle toward Tee. Bri passed her wife another vial.

"That's the last one," Bri said.

Sara emptied her first, switched to the next and continued. The circle was almost complete as Sara and Tee drew closer together.

Seeing their opportunity shrink, the infested surged and scrambled toward Tee and Sara and the remaining gap in the circle.

Jules swung his arm again, casting out more blazing droplets. "With St. Butler's blessing, you are denied entry!"

The droplets stung the spirits. Tendrils snapped away from affected areas as the blackened tissues flared with a golden light and crumbled away to specks that fell and faded. Each droplet broke the bonds of the *spirit eater* and a portion of the spirit dissolved. Some fell when limbs crumbled to dust. Others lost arms, or staggered with gaping rents in their bodies. It was enough to halt the surge, spirits climbing and piling on one another.

Tee and Sara came together and closed the circle. They stepped back and Tee pulled Sara into a hug.

Jules felt small arms suddenly grab him around the waist. He looked down and saw Mel hiding her face against him. She could see the spirits with her gift. The others looked around with darting eyes, maybe catching glimpses as the light flickered, but probably not seeing any of the gathered dead clearly.

The infested formed a wall around the circle that piled higher as they climbed one on another. The force of their hunger pushed them closer.

Then another ghost appeared in front of the infested spirits. It was the murdered girl, looking at him with dead eyes, her body nude and pale. She spread her arms out to her sides. The upside down cross-shaped wounds covering her body began to bleed.

"*Look what they did to me,*" she said.

The infested spirits behind her howled and reached for them. As the force of the crowd moved the legion closer, a golden light rose from around the circle. They screeched, the hideous tendrils shrinking back, pulling them like the puppet strings they were.

He pulled Mel away and passed her to Bri.

Jules shifted the vial to hold it with the Butlerian Bible, freeing his hand to reach into his exorcism kit. By feel, he found a bone bead and took it out.

He stepped forward to stand at the edge of the circle. He lifted the bead to his lips, kissed it, and said, "St. Butler preserve and protect this spirit, grant rest, and serenity."

He extended his hand, the bead flat on his palm out beyond the circle. Instead of pouncing, the infested hissed and drew back.

"Show me," he said to the ghost. "Show me what they did to you."

The ghost girl didn't draw back. She reached out and touched the bead with her finger.

"Oh," she said.

Her shape burst apart into fog, then swirled around in a funnel pointed at the center of the bead. The spirit vapors spun around, twirling down into the bead until they were all gone.

Jules pulled his hand back into the circle and clenched his hand into a fist around the bead.

The contact with the spirit knocked him to his knees.

"Jules?" Bri said.

"No," MAR-A said in a voice like the crack of a whip. "You must not touch him."

MAR-A knew the drill.

Images, feelings, and memories rushed into him through the spirit bead. They burned through him, setting his nerves on fire. It *hurt*.

St. Butler preserve and protect us, he said, soundlessly, and cradled his hand to his his chest.

Look what they did to me.

Jules looked. And experienced it with her.

Aubrey Jane. An exobiologist specializing in space-borne life working on the *Olympia.* Not quite as young as she looked, twenty-eight. Her first tour on the *Olympia.* They'd captured the comet, followed the usual procedures to measure and categorize the comet, probe its surface, and gathered samples.

A core sample came back with a piece of unusual red crystalline material.

Knives cut into her flesh, digging and gouging–

No. That came later. First it was the crystal piece in a core sample. The fragment no larger than a grain of rice. Unusual composition. Some process had to exist to create it. Maybe the comet came from a larger body with a liquid core.

Aubrey convince Captain Bouchard to use the arms to dig larger pits and authorize a boots -on-ice mission to gather more samples.

The second excavation broke into a large gas-filled pocket in the ice. Safety measures kept it from being evacuated into space.

"And damned them all." Aubrey wished those systems had failed. It could have saved her even if the outgassing might have damaged the ship.

A gas pocket was prime territory for an exobiologist. The sorts of things that might evolve through the comet's slow passages around the sun, it was a terrific opportunity.

She went with two repair bots to assist her.

Stepping into the cavern was like seeing a miracle as her suit lights illuminated the nearby surfaces she saw crosses. Hundreds, thousands of crosses from a few millimeters long to ones the length of her hand. The short ends stuck out of the ice, the two stubby arms bracing the structure, while the longer narrowing body stuck out into the space.

The light woke them. Triggered an active phase that must normally happen when the comet approached the inner system.

Blood-red and oxygen-starved blue tendrils extended out of the long bodies and waved through the gas, combing for the tiniest bits of life for spiritual energy.

Those closest to Aubrey found her. The tendrils wrapped around and then passed *through* her suit. Screaming, she lost her balance and fell among the crosses. More and more seized her. Took her. *Fed* on her and she was gone.

Knives cut into her, gouging her flesh around the crosses embedded there. Hands held her down.

"How'd they get through her suit?"

"Hell if I know!"

"We can't do this. It'll kill her."

"Space her."

It was too late. Aubrey couldn't tell them that. She couldn't warn them. Cursed them as they cut the crosses out. They kept cutting even as she expired–but by then those doing the cutting were infected already and continued the work to pass the crosses on to still living crew members.

Shutting down systems drove the crew into the habitat pod. Any that balked were driven there by the infected. A doctor, spared so far, retrieved her body and took it to the medical pod. It was a small kindness that the others repaid with an infection.

Jules sucked in a deep breath and shook as the experience left him shaking. Aubrey was quiet now. He'd seen what *they'd* done and understood that she didn't mean her desperate crew mates cutting the crosses out of her flesh. She had meant the *spirit eaters*. What they'd done, to her, and to the crew.

His breath escaped and he sucked it back. Jules unclenched his hand. The spirit bead had left marks on his palm. Later, if there was a later, he would braid it into his hair with the others that he kept close. The spirits contained rested with a measure of peace as long as they were with him.

Beyond the circle the *spirit eaters* piled and shrieked at him. Emaciated, blackened, sucked down to almost nothing–the *spirit eaters* had nearly consumed their hosts entirely. Now they wanted more. Him. The family. Eventually, if they could direct it, the *Olympia* would take them to the station or other inhabited port they could infest.

They were demonic, inhuman spirits. Parasitic. He had to stop them, somehow.

Chapter 38

NEED, HUNGER, AND RAGE drove the *spirit eaters* closer to the circle. It could not hold against so many for long if they came at it, but none wanted to be the first to sacrifice themselves.

Jules regained his feet and pocketed the spirit bead. He took up the vial of blessed water and the Butlerian Bible.

Bri still held Mel in her arms, Mel's faced buried in Bri's red hair and neck as she avoided looking at the *spirit eaters* around them. Sara stood resolutely between her parents, both hands clasped around a vial.

MAR-A stood ready at his side.

His options were limited. If he started the ritual of exorcism, nothing prevented the *spirit eaters* from fleeing. They could disperse themselves throughout the ship. He needed them all here.

He opened his feed connection to MAR-A and sent quick instructions. MAR-A acknowledge the burst.

Jules looked at the family. "You asked us here to help. That's what we're going to do. Listen to MAR-A."

He didn't have time for anything more. He stepped back out of the circle they'd created. His ears popped the moment he left it.

"No!" Bri said.

Jules turned as the massed *spirit eaters* surged like a wave about to wash over him. He flung his hand out in an arc, casting blessed water like a scythe in front of him.

"St. Butler preserves and protects us," he said.

The drops became burning stars that fell among the screeching *spirit eaters*. Tendrils retreated from the used husks they inhabited, leaving them to crumble to dust. It was too little to stop them all for more than a few seconds.

"With her blessing, we fear no evil." He lifted the Butlerian Bible higher. "Our spirits endure with her blessing. Evil holds no sway on us."

He walked forward and the *spirit eaters* retreated in a scramble in front of him while more filled the space behind him. The promise of a living host drove them to madness, to risk everything.

"St. Butler preserves and protects us and in Her name, I command you to release her children."

That was the signal MAR-A was waiting for. Abruptly, the force holding Jules to the floor vanished. He heard the others scream in shock and fear. The *spirit eaters* howled as they floated off the deck in all directions.

Jules released the empty vial and reached into the exorcism kit. He pulled out a handful of spirit beads and flung them out in an arc across his body. The movement of his arm spun him around, and he continued to throw spirit beads in all directions around the room.

Wailing like all of Hell was opening around them filled the chamber as each of the spirit beads opened as they touched the insubstantial remains of the former crew.

The *spirit eaters* didn't give up their hosts easily, even as they fragmented into the vortexes and were pulled into the bone beads. Tendrils snatched at the fragments of their hosts, trying to keep a grip on the pieces.

"St. Butler preserves and protects us," Jules said. His momentum carried him around. Tee, Bri, Mel, and Sara were safe–holding onto the stations on the deck. MAR-A stood with them. None of the failing *spirit eaters* were focused on them.

He turned his gaze up. Only stars showed in the window now. The *Olympia* was already out of view. MAR-A had ejected the command pod from the ship. Any of the pods could be released, inertia sending them off in a straight line from the rotating ship. Same as had happened with the first transit module.

He extended his arms to slow his rotation. The spirit beads were drawing in the remains of the former crew, allowing them to rest at last.

It left the *spirit eaters* exposed and stuck in the physical universe. Each crystalline cross gleamed as the pod lights activated. Their tendrils lashed, ineffectual at propelling them through the air.

"Now?" MAR-A sent along the feed.

Jules nodded. "Yes."

One of the crosses nearest to him, tendrils waving in his direction, suddenly flared bright and turned to white ash under the heat of MAR-A's plasma bolt.

More shots flashed around Jules, picking off any of the *spirit eaters* nearby first. He pulled in his arms, holding the Butlerian Bible to his chest. MAR-A's unerring continued.

Ships, stations, planets, moons, and even asteroids or comets provided oases in the void. The spiritual universe and the physical connected at such places. *Everywhere Life might arise, Life will arise in the span of the Universe.*

Without their hosts, the *spirit eaters* couldn't escape into the spiritual universe. They had no refuge from MAR-A's weapon. The spirit beads provided a safe haven for the remnants of the former crew's spirits. In time, those spirits might find peace.

One of the beads drifted within reach. Jules reached out and took it into his hand. The spirits within gave him only vague impressions of relief and gratitude.

"Be at peace," he said. "St. Butler watches over us. She preserves and protects us. You have nothing to fear."

Across the space of the pod, another *spirit eater* flared in a plasma bolt and turned to ash.

A second later a dark fluttering shape soared up to the balcony, caught it and perched there. MAR-A lifted an arm and took aim. Fired a plasma bolt. The former combat droid's eyes glittered with red lights in the shadows of its hood.

A few more minutes and Jules's trajectory brought him within reach of the third level balcony. He caught it and swung himself over to a station. He slipped, caught the seat, and pulled himself down. He fastened the belt across his lap.

Out in the open space, MAR-A jumped with unerring accuracy across the space. It used built-in jets to alter its trajectory. MAR-A landed in front of the station where Jules had strapped himself in. MAR-A's magnetic soles held it to the deck as it stalked forward.

"I have eliminated all visible targets," MAR-A said. It extended a hand, holding a bag that contained spirit beads. "I collected these."

Jules accepted the bag. He stored it in his exorcism kit. He would need to touch each and reassure the spirits contained. *Later.*

"We need to make sure none escaped before the *Olympia* arrives."

"I will take you," MAR-A said.

Jules allowed MAR-A to take him by the arm and guide him along.

With MAR-A's magnetic soles, they made good time around the level and Jules tried not to feel like a human balloon being tugged around. He extended his other sight, seeking any of the *spirit eaters* that had retreated into the spiritual universe.

The first was in a corner near the lift, barely perceptible as a darker presence in the thin shadows there. Jules lifted the Butlerian Bible.

"By Her name, I command you show yourself!" He exerted his will along with the command.

Whether it was the command, or the presence of a living host, the *spirit eater* exploded from its concealment.

Jules flicked a spirit bead into its path. "St. Butler preserves and protects us. Be at rest."

The form of the host dissolved into the vortex as it came into contact with the bead. Almost at the same time, MAR-A's other arm snapped up and the plasma weapon fired. The tumbling cross shape of the *spirit eater* was reduced to ash.

MAR-A deftly plucked the spirit bead out of the air and added it to a bag it produced from its robes.

"Hold that," MAR-A said to Jules, handing him the bag.

So it went, down through the levels of the command pod. Working as a team, they uncovered seven *spirit eaters*.

When the last was gone, Jules didn't get a sense of anything else in hiding.

They returned to the main floor where the family waited. Tee said, "Is that it? Did you get them?"

"Yes," MAR-A said.

Jules nodded and fought not to yawn. He was worn out. His bruises ached and his energy levels were low.

"When does the *Olympia* catch us?" Tee said, her tone angry. "How long do we have to work in zero gee?"

"I think it's neat," Mel said, bouncing against her straps. "I want to fly!"

Bri put a restraining hand on her. "Not here. When its safe, with help. You can still hurt yourself in zero gee."

Mel's face scrunched up. "But I can't fall?"

"You are falling," Sara said. "That's what this is. Everything is falling at the same rate around the sun. If you push off too hard it can still hurt when you hit a wall."

Mel seemed to consider that, then nodded. "Okay. I get it."

"Two days," MAR-A said. "Time was limited to plan the release. The *Olympia*'s engines are sufficient to intercept the pod. Onboard systems are equipped to maintain the environment."

"Except they haven't been tested," Tee said. "I'm going to have to check everything out."

"I have system access," MAR-A said.

"Yeah? That's great for anything the system can detect. Not so great for problems it can't."

Sara looked at Jules. "Is it safe? Are those things gone?"

Jules nodded. "I'm pretty sure. We'll stay alert, just in case."

Gone from the pod, but he could think of one more place where there were probably *spirit eaters* left.

Chapter 39

T HE TWO DAYS UNTIL rendezvous with the *Olympia* felt like a vacation. For some of them, at least. Tee spent much of the time checking over the systems.

Each pod was designed to be self-sufficient. At least for a time. It provided a safety factor that pods could be isolated. Or ejected from the ship's ring. The transit module had detached unexpectedly with no planning. In contrast, MAR-A had calculated the orbital trajectories so that *Olympia* could intercept the pod. Jules thought that two days was pretty good for a quick calculation.

Jules walked–thanks to magnetic boots they'd found in storage–to his chosen station on the main level. Everyone else was there, Sara and Mel at one station together. MAR-A and Bri occupying the next stations on each side around the circle. Tee sat strapped in at the center forward station.

He pulled himself down into the seat and fastened the lap strap that kept him in the seat. His station didn't have any active displays. He didn't need them. With his feed access he could see any data he wanted.

That didn't have his attention. What did was the holographic display that filled the central well of the command pod. It showed the *Olympia* on approach to the pod. The gap where the pod belonged looked like a missing tooth.

At the center of the *Olympia's* ring was the comet, the pits cut into the scarred surface showing where the harvester had occurred. Particles of ice liberated by sunlight floated around the comet in a sort of tenuous atmosphere. Behind it stretched the tail structure with the large drives and the widespread solar wings.

"Are we going to crash?" Mel said, voicing the tension that Jules felt.

He folded his hands and tried to project calm.

Tee grinned, a flash of teeth. "No, honey. MAR-A's calculations were right on point."

MAR-A shifted in its robe, but didn't say anything.

He caught Bri's eye, and they shared a smile.

The holographic display included overlays of the projected path. *Olympia's* speed and rotation meant the ring would come around precisely onto the pod's path to capture it.

Still, if the calculations were off at all, it could mean a disaster. He trusted MAR-A's aim. Any fear wasn't rational.

St. Butler preserve and protect us. He didn't voice the thought.

The moment, when it came, was slower than he'd expected. He transferred his attention to the window overhead where the *Olympia's* ring rolled slower and closer to the top of the pod. As the pod slid between the outer rails, magnetic guides brought the pod into the empty socket.

As soon as they connected with the ship, weight returned. He sank into the chair and found it comfortable. Weight settled on his lap, his chest, and for a second or two it felt like too much to bear.

That passed as his breathing settled. He lifted his hands—surprised a little at their weight—and clapped. Sara joined in, then Mel, Bri, and finally Tee. Everyone turned to look at MAR-A standing swathed in its robes. The former combat droid looked at them as if it thought they'd lost their minds.

"Docking achieved," MAR-A said, as a shudder ran through the pod. "All systems integration successful."

The clapping slowed and died away. Eyes turned toward Jules.

He unstrapped. "Let's get to the transit module. Follow us."

He started into the short corridor leading to the decon chamber. As he passed the baggage bot, he tapped its feed and told it to follow.

"Of course," it said in its cheerful voice.

They'd checked the command pod thoroughly in the two days it took to rendezvous. He was convinced that no *spirit eaters* remained. And although he suspected they had all been on the command pod when MAR-A ejected it, he couldn't be sure.

So they were taking the transit module back to their habitation pod. They'd check it first. If it checked out, they still had to check the other pods, but he suspected any spirits that remained were ordinary spirits like the one that Mel had channeled. Without the *spirit eaters* stirring things up, those were unlikely to be a problem.

He kept his other sight open and held a vial of blessed water in his hand as they went through the decon chamber into the transit module.

It checked out. Soon they were on their way back around the ring to the habitation pod. It gave him time to think over the plan they had developed over the past couple days.

The ERL had confirmed what he learned from Aubrey. The presence of the gas pocket in the comet, the crystalline cross-shaped lifeforms that had infested her. Her murder wasn't the crew's choice–the *spirit eaters* had done that and spread through the crew. They had fed and then rested, slowly consuming the crew's bodies and souls as the *Olympia* drifted.

A slight shake of his head rattled the spirit beads. It sounded different now, with so many new beads added. The touches of those new spirits were full of relief and gratitude. So much had been taken from them, but they had a chance to heal now in safety.

The comet remained the problem. They needed to know if any of the *spirit eaters* remained in the ice. His initial idea had been to send repair bots to investigate. MAR-A vetoed that with Tee's support. The spirits could influence the bots. MAR-A was their best option. Though not immune to influence, the droid was better equipped to handle what it found. Jules would give it his blessing before MAR-A went out there.

What to do if MAR-A found *spirit eaters* was a thornier problem. Cast the comet free, a potential hazard? Destroy the remaining *spirit eaters*? This was a unique form of life. It'd been necessary to destroy them to defend themselves on the command pod. Exterminating all of them would be a great sin, no matter how dangerous.

Sara had brought up the solution that they agreed on over breakfast the day before.

"Send it out of the galaxy," she said. "Out of the galactic plane."

It would take a long time for the comet to actually leave the galaxy, but MAR-A felt it could calculate an orbit that would eject the comet up out of the galactic plane. It would have to travel many light years but it could be done. The *spirit eaters* would continue on in their comet without coming close to another star. It would take many billions of years before the slow-moving comet would approach another galaxy.

There was no perfect solution, but Jules dared think that they would have St. Butler's approval.

Chapter 40

J ULES LOVED THE PRESS of people–of all species–
that filled the worship hall in the Butlerian Church on
the station. The noise of so many voices, the odors of
dozens of species, all mingled into something that told him
he was *home.*

He had taken his accustomed spot near the back of the
cathedral's hall, in a pew beside one of the enormous pillars
that rose to the high ceiling above. He'd only been back
three days, after spending a month with the Makkars on the
Olympia. It'd taken that long to get a ship out to pick up
him and MAR-A. The ship had also brought two
technicians that Bri had hired to help with her work and
the ship. They had a new comet to work with–MAR-A
had confirmed the presence of dozens of *spirit eaters*
remained in the pocket, with many more in other pockets.
They'd followed Sara's suggestion and sent that comet off in
an orbit to intergalactic space. He expected Bri's new
company would flourish and the crew complement would
grow.

It was good to be back. Other worshippers, seeing the
spirit beads in his hair, gave him space with respectful nods.

Mediums were not always accepted, though often in demand. It wasn't bad here.

A fael, a delicate-looking biped species, with legs that bent backwards, fine features, and large mobile ears, stopped at his pew. By the flowing dress and the dark tufts on the ears, he judged the fael male. To his other sight the fael was a void in the spiritual environment that enveloped him. They had no ghosts, no apparent continuation after life. It was a puzzle that remained unsolved, and one that vexed fael and non-fael scientists alike.

"Hello," the fael said. "May I join you?"

Jules indicated the seat beside him. "Of course. I am called Jules."

"Praetor," the fael said, touching its chest with long, multi-jointed fingers. "Thank you."

Praetor slipped gracefully past Jules and settled on the pew, legs folded up like a bird beneath the layers of cloth he wore. His wide, yellow eyes, looked around at the crowds, taking it all in.

"I have not attended a worship," Praetor confessed.

"Everyone is welcome," Jules assured him, wondering what brought the fael to the church.

"You are a medium, yes?" Praetor asked.

Jules nodded, then in case Praetor didn't understand the gesture, said, "Yes, that is correct."

"May we share a meal after the worship?" Praetor said. "I am seeking the assistance of a medium."

"Oh?"

Praetor fluttered his fingers. "Yes. It is a matter of, I believe the phrase is, a haunting?"

A haunting. From a fael? It might be interesting. "Alright," Jules said. "Let's talk over lunch after the worship."

"Thank you," Praetor said, folding his fingers. "This shall be most intriguing."

Jules shifted in the pew, unexpectedly eager for the worship to begin so it would be over sooner.

He wanted to know more about this haunting.

END

Be Readinary

Get a free short story collection when you sign up for my newsletter *READINARY*. Discover more exciting reads at readinary.com/crunch-bang

About the Author

Ryan M. Williams lives a double life as a full-time career librarian and a multi-genre writer with over twenty books. He writes across a range of genres including science fiction, fantasy, paranormal, mystery, horror, and romance. He earned a Master of Arts degree in writing popular fiction from Seton Hill University and a Master of Library and Information Science from San Jose University. His short fiction has appeared in Pulphouse Fiction Magazine, On Spec Magazine, and anthologies from Pocket Books and WMG Publishing.

To keep up with everything he creates, visit ryanmwilliams.com. Track his many series at their individual sites (FindingDeadThings.com, MoreauSociety.com.) He lives in Washington State with occasional forays into virtual reality.